Sonny

Sonny

JIM MILLER

DOUBLEDAY & COMPANY, INC.

GARDEN CITY, NEW YORK

1987

All of the characters in this book
are fictitious, and any resemblance
to actual persons, living or dead,
is purely coincidental.

Library of Congress Cataloging in Publication Data

Miller, Jim, 1945–
Sonny.

I. Title.
PS3563.I4125S6   1987   813'.54   86–24069
ISBN: 0-385-23257-8

For
Rose Adkins
Mentor, colleague and good friend

CHAPTER ONE

Turk didn't like him. It was as simple as that. But then, Turk didn't like many people anyway.

The tenderfoot got up off the floor, looked about the saloon as if to get his bearings, then squinted his eyes at the massive obstacle before him that was Turk Calder. That was when I knew Turk didn't like him. He jabbed hard at the kid's side, knocking the wind out of him, then brought down a huge right hand across the side of his face that floored him.

He was gamy, I'll give him that. Not too smart, but gamy. Most men fighting Turk would have laid there until he went back to his drinking, but not this Dennison kid. He rolled over and spit sawdust out of his mouth before Turk even had a chance to turn around. Then his face turned sheet white as Turk pulled out his six-gun and pointed it at him, a gravelly sound that was supposed to be a laugh coming from the big man.

"You shoulda stayed right there, pilgrim," he said. "You'd a been safer. Now I'm gonna kill you."

"No, Turk." It was one of the men beside him. "He ain't got a gun. It won't look good."

Turk's face changed expression—from pure pleasure to outright hatred. He seemed to turn red all over as he faced the other man. "Then someone give him one!" he yelled.

In an instant it was there, before the kid. As requested, someone had tossed a revolver onto the floor. And Turk, face still red, was smiling once more.

"Now he's got one," he said, and started to raise his arm, gun in hand, slowly bringing it down to bear on Dennison.

"I wouldn't do that, Turk," I said, leveling my shotgun at his midsection. "It's unhealthful." Now, I've never been that big a man, but you can believe that Greener brings an awful lot of respect when you're looking down the business end of it, and that's just what Turk was dealing with. In fact, as soon as his friends spied that shotgun, it got real vacant around that bar. I was standing just inside the bat-wing doors and to the right, my back to the wall, and there was no one in that part of the saloon now but me, the kid and Turk.

"You stay outta this, Dallas." As he said it, he turned his face toward me, but that was the only part of him that moved. He still had his Colt pointed at the kid, and Dennison still looked like he was waiting for the undertaker to shovel the dirt in over him. "This ain't your affair. Just me and the kid."

"Wrong, Turk." I was getting mad, but like I say, Turk had a way of doing that to you. "He's my passenger, and Mr. Chisum said to take care of him." I threw a disgruntled glance at this Dennison youngster, wishing I knew how this incident had gotten started. "And right or wrong, I will," I said, remembering how far back me and John Chisum went.

"I could kill you, Dallas, you know that." There was a little line of sweat forming on Turk's brow now and he didn't sound so sure of himself. I hoped he was bluffing.

"No you won't," I said, in a tone that let him know right off that I meant business. "Oh, you might shoot me, Turk, but you'll never know whether or not you killed me." When I cocked the second hammer I realized how quiet it was, for it was the only sound in the room. But it was Turk's eyes I was watching, and when I pulled back that second hammer I had him and he knew it. " 'Cause when I pull the triggers on this Greener, there ain't gonna be enough of you left to make sonofabitch stew."

It did the trick and a look of relief came over Dennison's face and Turk eased the hammer down on his weapon and holstered it. At the same time he turned so red in the face that I thought he would bust a blood vein any second. Without looking at anyone else in the room, he headed for the saloon doors, started to push one bat-wing open and stopped briefly to face me.

"It ain't over yet." The way he said it left little doubt that he figured on settling with me sometime in the future.

"Of course not," I said with a smile of my own. It wasn't until he was out the door that I lowered the shotgun.

"One round on the house, boys," the bartender boomed, and most of the patrons used that excuse to belly up to the bar.

I walked over to where the pilgrim was getting up, cocked an eye at him to survey the damage. "You all right?"

"I guess." He was either shy or still had the wind knocked out of him because I could barely hear him. Or maybe he was just plain scared. No one would blame him for that after what he had just been through.

"Abe, let me have a couple of beers over here," I yelled at the barman. Then I found a corner table and pulled out a couple of chairs for us as the kid half-staggered behind me. I took the seat with the wall to my back, something a lot of men were doing after learning of what happened to Hickok, and laid the scattergun on the table. We sat there in silence until the beer came, and I used the time to study the features on this young lad.

He was tall but a bit on the light side, sort of like an eighteen-year-old who hasn't had a chance to fill out yet. And that was what must have happened in this boy's case, at least from what I had overheard John and his niece say. But I should've guessed he was in for trouble, or would be, as soon as anyone saw him wearing those city clothes and a bowler hat. Not even John Chisum would have gotten away with wearing a hat like that without some funning.

When the bartender set the beers down he gave a sidelong glance at the kid, shook his head in disbelief.

"Yup, you guessed it, Abe," I said with a smile, for I knew he was thinking the same as I. "A sure enough mail order catalogue on foot."

"Sir?" the lad said as the bartender walked off.

"Don't call me that, sonny," I said. "I work for a living." If I sounded disgusted when I said it, I was, for I had never had any respect for apple polishers and figured that anyone starting to call you "sir" was doing just that. I pushed back my hat and drank half the beer at one swallow. I took in the kid's features again, noticed some blood starting to flow from his nose and dug in my pocket for a kerchief. "Here," I said, tossing it to him, "wipe yourself off 'fore you bleed to death." He grabbed the oversized cotton cloth and I chuckled to myself again. "A tenderfoot, all right. Green behind the ears and bloodied up front."

He wiped the corner of his mouth and nose, then noticed the blood that was spattered here and there on his fancy suit. The look on his face showed the disappointment he felt now that it was ruined.

"Just as well," I said, "you wear duds like that in Lincoln County and you won't last out the year lest you go into hiding."

Without comment he reached for the beer, stopped in mid-motion, his arm frozen in place only inches from the handle of the beer mug. His face grimaced in pain, but he didn't say a word.

"Ribs, huh?"

"I think so," he said, slowly taking a drink.

"You'll be all right," I said, taking another swallow of my own drink. These folks from back East tended to think you were real uncaring if you passed off something like this without fussing over them, but bruises and busted bones were a way of life once you got past the Mississippi, and we seldom gave them a second thought. "What I want to know, Dennison, is how this fandango got started."

"Woodrow," he said, half-smiling. "Please call me Woodrow."

"Woodrow?" I found myself shaking my head in the same disbelief the bartender had. "Woodrow? Good Lordy, boy, did your parents hate you *that* much?" I finished my beer and silently waved for two more, then remembered that even on the ranch I had never been introduced to this youngster. "By the way, my name's Haywood, Dallas Haywood." He took another sip of his beer, squinting at me. "You still got your memory, still remember coming from the Chisum spread?"

Whatever else he was feeling, he must have just wanted to be left alone, for he ignored the question. "Look, Mr. Haywood, I think I'll—" he said, starting to rise. But just like reaching for that beer, the pain stopped him and he fell more than sat back down, the same look of agony crossing his face.

"Keep your seat, sonny. You ain't going nowhere." I reached into my hip pocket, pulled out a flask and tossed it across the table. "Here, take some of this. It'll ease the pain."

"What is it?"

"Medicinal."

He eyed the pint-sized container suspiciously, but he finally gave in and took a good healthy swallow, knowing there wasn't much else that was within reach to ease the pain. I smiled as he took the drink, remembering how I had reacted to my first slug of Taos Lightning. Once it hit rock bottom it started a fire in your stomach that seemed to bypass everything and go directly to your brain. Now, if you let it settle, it has a sort of warming effect on you. But this young buck must have thought he had to put the fire out and made the mistake of swallowing half of that second beer to do it. The beer was only fuel for the fire and I smiled at the look on his face, thinking he would breathe fire any minute.

"You tried to poison me!" he blurted out in a hoarse voice.

"Hell, no. That's Taos Lightning. Best for whatever ails you."

"But, it's—"

I nodded. "Two hundred proof," I said, trying not to sound as though there were too much pride in my voice. "Homemade. Takes the paint off your deck if you got a boat." Then, with a chuckle, I added, "Not that you'll ever find one in the New Mexico Territory."

The liquor was taking effect, for he had calmed down some and slowly sipped at the rest of his beer.

"Now, sonny," I said in a more serious tone, "since I almost killed a man with this thing"—I lifted the shotgun I had laid across the center of the table, set it gently back down—"maybe you'd like to explain why. I gotta tell you that I'm godalmighty curious."

"Surely." He said it slowly, squinting at me as though he were having trouble seeing me. "I simply came in here, as you suggested, and got a drink. I struck up a conversation with the gentleman at the bar and mentioned that I had brought Miss Margaret to her friend's ranch." He stopped, the pain suddenly gone as a moon-eyed look came over his face, the kind I had seen before on more than one young lad in puppy love. And thinking back on Margaret Dawson, the pretty young lady he had escorted to the Chisum ranch, I couldn't say as I blamed him. She couldn't have been any older than this Dennison character, but she was a looker for sure.

"She's nice, don't you think?" he said with a lopsided grin.

Then he squinted at me one more time, and passed out . . .

CHAPTER TWO

"And that's about it, John. The damn fool kid must've taken offense to hearing this girl called a whore and decided to be chivalrous. At least that's what I got in bits and pieces on the way back to the ranch."

Woodrow Dennison was stretched out on a bed in one of John Chisum's guest rooms. I was trying to doctor the boy up and at the same time explain to my boss just why I had to. After he passed out I had to put him in the back of the buckboard and listen to him mumble about the events of the morning. John wasn't any too happy about what had happened and was just getting a good bite on my backside, chewing me out and wanting to know how I could let it take place, when I told him about Turk Calder and how he had started the fight in the first place. John eased up some then because even he knew how worthless Turk and his kind were. Especially in the feuding that had gone on of late.

I applied some liniment to the right side of the boy's rib cage and he was all of a sudden very much alive, groaning and wincing at the same time.

"So you're not going to die on us, huh?" John said with a smile. He had a way with people like that, John did. It could be the hardest of times and he would still come up with a laugh and a smile for you, almost as if he were treating the world and its events lightly.

"No, sir," the boy said, trying to force a smile. "I don't think so."

"You sure you're gonna be all right?" John asked. "That looks like an awful tender spot you've got there."

"Hell, boss, there ain't nothing wrong with him," I said, a bit taken by how John was babying this youngster. "Besides, you know how these young squirts are. Don't take 'em no time to heal."

The prospect of being called a squirt didn't set well with Dennison and I think if he hadn't been in the pain that he was he would have come charging right off the bed at me. As it was, he turned a shade of red not too far from what I'd seen on Turk Calder's face that morning, forced himself to sit up before making a charge at me. And sick or not, he might well have, had it not been for John's hand coming to rest on his shoulder to hold him in place.

John knew how I felt about upstarts, especially these young ones that kept showing up out West with some mythical idea of what fun cowboying was. After a while you can spot them and Woodrow Dennison had the dress for it without a doubt. From what I'd seen of the boy that day the only credit I was about to give him was for persistence. Not much in the line of brains, but he was persistent.

After a long pause, John reached in his pocket, pulled out a watch fob and checked the time, his hand still steady and resting on Dennison's shoulder. In a more serious tone he glanced at the boy, then turned to me. "About time for chuck, wouldn't you say, Dallas?"

"Right, boss. I'll get right to it." John knew as well as I that there was a good hour before I would even have to start cooking, but I went along with him anyway, knowing he was trying to keep down the friction between me and this new lad. Anyway, the supplies needed unloading and I was the only one there to do it, so it wouldn't be wasted time.

As I walked out the door and down the hallway, I heard John say, "You sit tight, Mr. Dennison. I'll get Sallie up here in a bit to patch you up."

To the men of the Jinglebob spread he was "Uncle John," and I never could figure out why. Maybe it was because Miss Sallie had called him that from the day she arrived and added a woman's touch to the house. Most likely it was because John Chisum just acted like the uncle that some of us never had. He wasn't like a lot of the big ranchers who sat back and let their foreman run the outfit while they counted the profits. Not John. The time he wasn't at the main ranch house he was out on the range with his men, working the herds or fixing up what needed doing. One of his favorite stories was about the drifter passing through who came upon Uncle John working at a chore on the ranch, wearing a battered old straw hat, overalls and heavy brogan shoes. The stranger figured him for one of the hired hands. "Working for Old Chisum?" he asked in a somewhat condescending tone.

John only looked up at the man with that grin of his. "Yes," he said. "Working for Old Chisum."

I was remembering that old story as I headed for the front door when I heard a small voice off in the far corner. It wasn't unusual to find strangers in the Chisum house, and I would have kept right on going, but for the urgency in what was being said.

"Sir?" It was the young lady that Dennison had brought out from back East. She got up from her seat and I never will know how she could walk that fast in as fancy a getup as she wore. But there she was at my side, a worried look on her face. "Is he all right? Is he hurt badly?"

"No, ma'am," I said, grabbing my hat off my head and taking in her features. "Nothing a good dose of liniment won't cure." She had the kind of hair Miss Sallie would have called auburn. It made the fair skin of her face seem lighter than it was, but it was her eyes that caught my interest. They had a newborn's innocence and something else I couldn't quite place but had seen before some time long ago.

"You find that humorous, mister whatever-your-name-is?"

"Huh? Oh no, ma'am," I said, suddenly aware that I was smiling, more to myself than to her. "It's not funny at all, him getting hurt and all." I tried my best to say it with a straight face, but couldn't keep from smiling at her, finally speaking what was on my mind. "It's just that . . . well, ma'am, I reckon I'd have fought over you, too, if'n I knew you was this pretty."

I had to say it quick to get it out, for conversing with women wasn't my strong suit. I was starting to feel the red crawl up my neck when I noticed that this young lady was already red-faced.

"He did that?" she said in surprise. "He got into a fight over me?" She sounded as if no man had ever paid any attention to her, something I doubted considerably.

"Well, yes, ma'am. If'n you're the Miss Margaret . . . I mean, Miss Dawson, that he's been telling me about." I said it wishing Miss Sallie was there, knowing she could say things that came out right. Or Kate. At least I knew them, but this girl was enough to tangle tongue any man and I didn't feel comfortable around her at all.

"Yes," she said with a smile. "I am she. And you are—?"

"The biscuit shooter," I said automatically. "That is . . . Haywood, Dallas Haywood. Yes, ma'am, that's it." I just plain couldn't talk right around her and half expected her to bust out laughing. "That is, I'm the cook for this lash up . . . ranch, I mean." I had to get out of there and fast. "And, ma'am, I've got a lot to do, so if you'll excuse me," I said, and all but ran out the door.

I sloshed the hat back on my head and was halfway to the cookshack when I saw Tom Lang approaching from the corral.

"Don't say a word, Lang," I yelled at him. "Just get me

one of them loafers you call a cowhand, so's I can get these supplies unloaded. Leastwise, if you want to eat tonight."

"I tell you, John, it can't go on like this," I said. It was getting close to sundown and Chisum and Miss Sallie were seated on the veranda, taking in the colors that looked best at that time of day. Me, I had other things on my mind. "Why, do you know they was complaining about the food tonight again? Said it was too late a-coming, didn't taste right!"

But he only grinned. "Dallas, you know good and well there isn't a ranch hand born that didn't complain about the grub he was served, no matter how good it was."

I never did get the man to help me unload the buckboard that afternoon and wound up serving the ranch hands a bit later than usual. I had to admit that what John said was right about a cowhand bellyaching about the quality of the food he was eating, but that was all part of ranch life and I didn't mind it at all, for it showed that they were at least paying attention to what you did for them. It was when they got to voicing gripes that you got to wondering if they were just doing their regular grumbling or if you maybe ought to start taking them seriously. And I would have told John that if I hadn't been interrupted by the Dennison kid and the Dawson girl joining the Chisums on the porch. They were smiling at one another, all moon-eyed and such, and I figured that any minute they would take to holding hands, but they were too excited for that.

"Well, now," John said. "You sure are looking right happy for a fella that didn't think he'd make it through the afternoon." Then he smiled and there was mischief in his eye when he winked at the boy and eyed the girl as he spoke. "Of course, I don't reckon I'd be paying much attention to any pains I had if I was escorting someone as pretty as you, Miss Dawson."

When the two of them blushed, John and I had a good

laugh before Sallie stepped in and tried to make them feel at ease.

"Oh, don't mind them," she said, going to the girl's side. "Why, Uncle John does that to everybody and Dallas"—she paused for a moment, shooting a warning glance in my direction—"well, Mr. Haywood just seems to do it on general principles."

John grinned and shook his head at me while the two youngsters got their composure back. When they did, it was Miss Margaret who spoke first. There was a renewed excitement in her voice as she took one of Sallie's hands in both of hers.

"Woodrow's going to stay, Sallie. Isn't that wonderful?" It may not have been intended as a surprise, but that's what it was to the Chisums. When she saw the frown of suspicion on John's face, she added, "With your permission, of course, Mr. Chisum."

"Well, I reckon we can always use another good hand."

"Oh, he'll be that, Mr. Chisum," she replied. "I just know he will." All the time she was speaking, I saw her gazing that cow-eyed stare at Dennison and I couldn't help but feel that if this kid did decide to stick around, it would be more for the young lady than anything else. One thing I knew for sure, and that was that when a man started courting a woman, she generally had him doing for her in no time. And it didn't take much to see that she had this gangly young lad bridled for a good start because he hadn't spoken yet.

"That right, Mr. Dennison?"

"Yes, sir," the boy said, coming out of his trance or whatever it was that had his tongue locked up. "I'd sure like to give it a try."

"You would, huh?" John said it more to himself than to anyone else, sizing up Dennison in one glance. Then he turned to the Dawson girl. "Margaret, would you mind giving Sallie a hand for a minute? I think she's got some-

thing that's a good drink for this time of evening out back
in the kitchen." When the women were gone, he motioned
a hand to an empty chair. "Young man, why don't you have
a seat." When I turned to go, John stopped me with, "No,
hang on a minute, Dallas. You're as good as family here.
Wait just a minute."

I shrugged, still leaning against a corner post.

"Now, then, Mr. Dennison—"

"Please call me Woodrow, sir."

"WOODROW," I scowled, the disgust on my face match-
ing the tone of my voice.

"Yes, sir," he said indignantly. "And what's wrong with it,
may I ask?"

"Oh, nothing," I said, "if you can explain—"

"Gentlemen," John broke in, "I don't really care about
names right now." Glancing back at Dennison, he continued. "Can you ride?"

"Some." He was hesitant now.

"Can you shoot?"

Dennison's spirits brightened. "I was the best shot on our
team with a sporting gun."

"That so?" A hint of a frown began to form on John's face.
"Ever work cattle, do anything on a ranch?"

"No, sir. But I'd like to try."

"Son," John said, slowly shaking his head. "Do you know
what's brewing out here? Do you know what you're getting
yourself into? I see how you look at that young girl, and I
can't say as I blame you. But if you're just doing it for the
sake of that girl, just to impress her—"

"Oh no, sir," the boy said, trying to sound reassuring.
Then he blushed, smiled shyly. "I won't deny that I've
taken a fancy to Margaret and that I like her. And I think
she likes me, too. But I've been watching the people out
here ever since we left St. Louis and I like them. They're
different than those I grew up with in the East. They're—"

"More dangerous, sonny." When he looked at me, confused, John took over.

"What Dallas means is that this land is wilder than most of what you've seen. And I'm afraid, son, that you've wandered into one part of it that's wilder than most at the moment. That's why I asked if you knew what you were getting into."

"I don't understand." The boy was still confused.

"I'm talking about a war, Mr. Dennison, a shooting war. It probably doesn't make any sense to people like you, but the men who fought so hard to get and keep this land . . . well, they're fighting each other now to get their neighbors' land as well. There's a good amount of politics and greed involved in it." He cocked a curious eye toward the lad. "Are you certain you still want to stay?"

"Yes, sir." He said it with pride and I somehow got the feeling that he was determined to make a go of it out here, whether the girl had anything to do with it or not. If he knew just how dangerous the game we were playing was, he didn't show it. But then, he would find out soon enough.

"All right, Woodrow. You can officially consider yourself as one of the hands. Can you take orders?"

"Yes, sir, Mr. Chisum," he said enthusiastically.

"Good." Then Uncle John looked at me, a mischievous smile on his face as he spoke. "Starting tomorrow, you'll be working with Mr. Haywood here as his assistant."

Dennison was as surprised as I was.

"But, sir, I thought—"

"I know what you thought, Mr. Dennison, just like every tenderfoot that comes out here. Well, right now Dallas is short on help, so you consider him your boss from now on, and if you work out with him we'll see about making you a bonafide cowhand with some work on the spread."

"Yes, sir," the boy said in a dejected manner.

I wasn't sure if John was playing a trick on me or if he actually expected me to make something out of this kid, but I wasn't about to argue with him. I knew him better than that.

The sun was down now and the women hadn't returned from the kitchen yet, probably palavering over something, I figured. I planted my hat on my head, said good night to John and gave a short glance at Dennison.

"Better get to bed, sonny. From now on, your days are gonna start right early."

CHAPTER THREE

"Come on, sleeping beauty," I said, shaking his shoulder for the third time. He rolled over, grumbled something to himself and focused his eyes on me.

"What? What time is it? It's still dark." He pulled the blanket back up to his shoulder and would have gone back to sleep if I had not pulled it clear off of him.

"It's time for us to go to work, sonny," I said through grit teeth. "Now, I don't care if you got a hankering to work in nothing but your drawers, but I'd advise you to get something on and be at the cookshack in about two shakes."

I stomped out and headed back to the shack and began making the fixings for breakfast. The kid was right, it was still dark, somewhere around three-thirty I gauged. I never did have a watch or a clock, for the timing and such came natural to a man after he had been cooking long enough. Even the getting-up time. It was like something inside just gave you a poke in the ribs when it was time and, drunk, sober, sick or damn near dying, you hauled your carcass out of the bunk.

I had two fires going when the kid came in, one in the potbellied stove and one in the oven.

"You start this early?" he asked in astonishment, rubbing his eyes.

"Ary day," I said. "There's water out back. You throw some on you and then get back here and pay attention. We got plenty to do." When he came back I pointed to the case of Arbuckles in the corner and told him to make the coffee for starters. If there was nothing else on hand, a good cook always had his coffee ready, any time of the day.

"I'm sorry, Mr. Haywood," he shrugged, blushing a bit. "But I'm not much of a cook."

"Well, we're gonna fix that right now, sonny," I said. "You just fill that pot with water and throw in a sack full of Arbuckles and let 'er boil a half-hour or so."

"But how can you tell if it's done?"

"When time's up, throw in a horseshoe. If it floats, it's done, if it don't, it needs to boil another half-hour." When he gave me a look that said he didn't know whether to believe me or not, I smiled. "A half-hour's good, son, take my word for it."

It wasn't long afterward that Tom Lang came in and poured himself some coffee. He was as big as Chisum, but a bit beefier in his chest and shoulders. He had worked with Uncle John for a couple of years as a cowhand, but when the people in Lincoln County started getting serious about shooting one another, he proved he could handle a gun as well as a rope and John had put him in charge of the boys on the range.

"I tell you, cookie, there ain't a better way to start a day than with a good cup of coffee," he said, taking his first bold gulp of the steaming liquid. "Yup, you always have made good coffee."

"Now, Tom, you know better'n to try and smooth talk me," I said, "so just speak what's on your mind. Besides," I added, as my assistant came in with another armful of firewood, "he's the one made it." The boy put the wood in the corner of the far side of the room and I motioned him over. "Tom, meet my new helper, Woodrow Dennison."

Lang stuck out a huge paw that all but engulfed the lad's own fist, the same disbelieving look coming to his face as had mine when I first heard the boy's full name. "Woodrow?"

"Yes, sir." The lad was almost cringing from Lang's grip.

"Howdy." Then, looking at me, he smiled. "Does he know what the boys are gonna do to him with a monicker like that?"

It was plain to see that the boy was getting tired of being told about his name, and for a minute he got real feisty about it. "Excuse me," he said to Lang, a scowl forming on his face, "but is there something wrong with my name? All I seem to hear about it are wiseacre remarks which I frankly do not like."

He was headed for a sure run-in with the foreman, a losing one at that, and it crossed my mind that this must've been how he had gotten into the fight with Turk Calder, too. Whatever it was, he was the only help I had and I wasn't about to lose him on his first day before breakfast had even been served.

"All right, you birds, that's enough," I said, fed up with them. "There's work to do here, yet. Sonny, I need a hell-uva lot more firewood than that," I said, glancing at the small stack in the corner.

"Look, Haywood, if you think I'm gonna take any backtalk from some tenderfoot—"

"I don't give a damn what you think, Lang," I said as I brought up the cleaver in my hand. "You may be the top screw out on the range, but once you step in here, you're in my domain. Now, you didn't just come in to praise my belly-wash, so let's have it."

He wasn't one to back down, but he knew I was dead serious about who was the boss in the kitchen. And I could tell by the expression on his face that he was none too fond of that oversized knife in my hand. So all of a sudden he got real civil.

"I'm taking about a dozen of the hands out east to the Pecos to round up some strays. It'll be an all-day ride and I wondered if I could get some Injun bread and beef for noon camp."

"It'll be ready when you are," I said, and started to turn

back to the oven when I noticed Dennison, scowl still on his face, glaring at the foreman. "Sonny," I said, not yet over the mad I felt, "I ain't in the habit of repeating myself. Now, you get me that firewood and I mean pronto."

I gave an abrupt glance to both of them and each left the kitchen, Lang gulping the rest of his coffee and the gangly youngster sullenly walking toward the rear of the cook-shack.

It was an hour later when I rang the triangle and yelled "Fall to" for the benefit of those hands who hadn't made it to the community table yet. I had the boy setting down plates of flapjacks with a side of beef for good measure, when the men started whispering among themselves and giving strange looks to Dennison.

"Boys," I said, tapping the side of the coffeepot with my knife to get their attention. "I want you to meet my new assistant. Now, he's brand new out here, but I expect it won't be too long afore he's cooking for you all by his lonesome, so you treat him right."

"You mean, we're actually gonna get meals on time, now?" one hand yelled out from the far end of the table.

"Well, what's his name?" another asked.

I looked back at Dennison standing in front of the oven, a sheepish grin on his face, and somehow I just couldn't do it. I had to admit that the boy had pitched right in, even if what he did was only basic chores, so I couldn't bring myself to tell them he was Woodrow Dennison.

"Sonny," I said. "Yeah, Sonny's his handle."

He seemed more confused than anything when several of the men called out "Hi, Sonny," and welcomed him to the ranch in their own offhand way. After he was through setting plates down, I spelled him so he could eat, but even back in the corner his face was a livid red the rest of the meal.

Shortly after the last of the men left, Lang showed up and I handed him a possibles sack with his noon meals in it.

"You see any deadwood out that way, I'd appreciate it if you'd pick some up," I said. When he frowned, I added, "You know what the rule is," and jerked a thumb over my shoulder at a crude piece of wood I'd hung above the entrance to the cookshack. There were enough duties to perform around there to keep any three cooks busy, but some of the hands seemed to have the idea that I had nothing to do between meals and should collect my own firewood. So I had fashioned the sign above the doorway as a reminder of what was expected of anyone who liked getting three squares a day. "NO FUEL—NO FOOD" the sign pronounced and the boys took it to heart, for it was seldom that I ran out of firewood.

"I'll see what I can do."

"Obliged," I said. Then, as an afterthought, "He's young, Tom. Give him time." He didn't reply, but I had the feeling that what friction there had been between us earlier was gone when he shrugged noncommittally before riding off.

Inside, I set my new helper to washing the tin plates and what passed for silverware as I began checking my stocks for additional shortages. The trip the day before had only been to pick up immediate needs, but now that I had someone to help me, I could load and unload in half the time and still be on time for the evening meal. Making the list didn't take long and it was when I'd finished that I noticed the same sullen look that had appeared on the boy's face earlier when I chewed him out about the firewood. I grabbed a towel and wiped and replaced a few of the plates, but he said nothing.

"All right, pilgrim," I said a bit impatiently. "Let's hear it."

"Sir?" he said, looking up.

"Dallas, boy. The name is Dallas. And it don't take much to see that you've got more on your mind than a hat, so let's hear it."

He hesitated a moment, then finally decided to talk.

"It's just the name, sir . . . uh, Dallas. What's wrong with my name? I've always been proud of it and—"

"Look, son," I said. "That's fine and good, but out here you're dealing with a different breed of men and a whole new way of life. It's . . . well, you've got to fit the land, and believe you me, it's hard enough surviving out here without having to fight over what your name is.

"Besides, it's kind of a custom out here, naming things." He didn't say anything, instead set what he had back in the water and listened closely to what I said. "The people that come out here, well, they named the land and the rivers and the mountains and . . . well, they just started naming the people, too. And Lang was right, you know."

"Oh?"

"Hell, yes," I said, waving a hand off to one side. "Why, if I hadn't give you that name, you'd have been so busted up at the end of the day from fighting that you wouldn't do me or Uncle John any good on this ranch. You think on it."

I left him to finish washing the dishes while I hitched up the buckboard and told Uncle John that Dennison and I would be gone until early afternoon getting supplies in Lincoln. When I returned, the boy was throwing some Arbuckles into a fresh watered pot. He threw in an extra piece of firewood and said, "That ought to hold 'em for the morning." It seemed like his disposition had changed some for the better.

"Not bad, son. You're catching on."

Most times I usually enjoyed the ride into Lincoln to pick up supplies. It gave a person time to think, and when you put up with complaining cowboys and the sound of pots and pans hitting one another all day, well, you learn to appreciate the silence of a ride alone. But that wasn't going to happen with the Dennison kid along for a companion. He was worse than most women at a Sunday social, trying to find out just what was going on in the territory. Or else he actually did have an interest in the people of this land like he said. But it was the newfound violence in Lincoln County, what some were beginning to call the Lincoln County War, that he was most interested in.

"What did Mr. Chisum mean by a shooting war, Dallas?"

"Just that," I said. "One thing about people out here, Sonny, that makes 'em more dangerous than most."

"What's that?" he asked eagerly, not even noticing my use of the nickname I'd given him.

"When they get tired of talking, it ain't too awful unusual that they start shooting. 'Specially when they get pushy with their words. A man can only take so much." It was evident that I had his attention now.

"It was '71 when Uncle John gave up delivering contracted beef for Charlie Goodnight and set up his own spread out here. I never was much good with numbers except when it come to making sure I had enough powder and ball, but I'll tell you, son, I'd wager the Jinglebob spread runs a good hundred and fifty miles from one corner to another."

Sonny gave a low whistle of admiration before he got curious again. "But, what about the war?"

"Well, Lincoln County has always been known for a lack of law, and Uncle John had to handle his share of it by himself until '75 when a fella named McSween showed up. At first he was pretty much a loner but then this Englishman, Tunstall, bought himself a ranch the year after."

"I don't understand. What do they have to do with the war?"

"I reckon you've got to understand that if it wasn't for beef contracts to the government, the ranchers, big and small, wouldn't make much of a go around here. And if they don't make a profit, neither do the merchants. Knowing that, a couple of fellas named Murphy and Dolan opened up a mercantile in Lincoln and started bidding on contracts for delivery of beef to the government at the same time. They figured to buy cheap and sell high and get control of the local farmers and ranchers by getting 'em in debt to 'em. Somehow or other they got the backing of politicians in Santa Fe and pretty soon they owned the law and everything else around.

"Anyway, McSween and Tunstall got as tired of it as Uncle John and formed their own mercantile in Lincoln and managed to get the support of the small farmers and ranchers. Rumor had it that Dolan was dealing in stolen cattle to fill his contracts and the McSween-Tunstall faction got even more support."

"That all sounds very interesting, Dallas," the boy said impatiently, "but what about the war? When did it start?"

"Well, most folks will tell you that the talking stopped and the shooting started a month or so back when a so-called posse of Dolan's men murdered Tunstall. The sheriff arrested Fred Waite and the Kid for it, but everyone knows they worked for Tunstall so they had no call to shoot him."

"The Kid?"

"Oh," I said, remembering who it was I was telling this story to. "I forgot, you're new here. Some call him Billy the Kid. Some call him Billy Bonney. Dolan tagged him for a killer, and he's not far off."

"How's that?"

"Well, I don't think the Kid done in Tunstall 'cause the man treated him like he was his own son. But you stay clear of him, Sonny. He ain't no older than you but he's a man killer for sure. You mark my words. I've seen men like him before and death just has a way of following 'em, no matter where they go. You stay clear of him."

"But what happened to him? The way you talk, they must have let him go."

"They had to. No hard evidence to hold him on."

"Well, where is he now, this Billy the Kid?"

I scratched my jaw, realized the stubble on it was at least

two days' old and that I should have took the time to shave. After all, I was going to be seeing Kate.

"Last I heard, he taken four or five men and went back to Tunstall's outfit, saying he was gonna protect the women and kids out there from the likes of Dolan and his men."

I had taken my time during the ride to make sure I had everything down right and we were approaching the edge of town when I finished up.

"Just one thing, Dallas." The boy seemed hesitant.

"What now?" I said irritably. I had given up a chance for the only solitude I could find around the Chisum ranch in order to fill in this tenderfoot on just what was going on, and here he still was not satisfied.

"How do you know all this stuff?"

It was not the question I thought he would ask, and I found myself smiling at the thought of it.

"That, Sonny, is something you find out right soon when you take to being a cook," I said, still smiling.

"What's that?"

I leaned toward him, as though to whisper the ingredients of some secret recipe. "You're gonna learn more about the people and the country at a cookshack community table than any of them old hens ever gossip about in town."

When he laughed, I was not certain if it was directed at the humor of it or the unbelievability of it, but somehow I got the idea he thought I was stretching the blanket some.

Lincoln was not one of those towns people kept talking about out West that had sprung up "overnight." The only one I could remember having ever done that in the Southwest was Tombstone, and that only because it was the center of a mining strike. Besides, most of the buildings in this part of the country were made from adobe and it took more than "overnight" for adobe to set when you were making with it.

The main road, which was the only road, going through

town ran from east to west, parallel to the Rio Bonito in back of the buildings on the north side of town. The sight of a tree here and there was enough to give a body the feeling he was coming on civilization compared to a lot of the barren land in the territory. We passed the jail on the outskirts of town and I pulled up in front of the Montano store that Kate worked in. It was a general merchandise store, and other than Tunstall mercantile, I picked up a lot of my goods there.

When I tied the reins to the hitch rack, I noticed that Dennison was still sitting on the buckboard, only he was staring at the building next to the Montano store. It was Ike Stockton's Saloon, where Turk Calder had taken a dislike to him the day before.

"Forget it, Sonny. I don't like Turk any more'n you do, but this is strictly business today," I said.

The inside of the store had everything you would expect of a general store, from a coffeepot to the beans to go in it, and I noticed the kid taking it all in with a new interest.

"So you did come back." The voice was a deep one for the woman it came from. Kate stood behind the counter, the ever-present smile on her face. She reminded me some of John Chisum because where John was constantly laughing or joking, Kate had a smile for everyone, and I was one of the few that knew that each one did it to cover up some tragedy in their life. "I heard about the ruckus next door yesterday and did not know if you'd be coming in for that second load or not."

"You know better'n that, Kate," I said. "I didn't come in and get 'em, Uncle John'd have my hide nailed to the wall, tanned and cured."

"And who's this?" she asked, noticing my companion.

"This is the young man who caused the ruckus you heard about. Woodrow Dennison meet Kate Rogers," I said, introducing the two. "He's my new assistant," I said. I added, "Don't argue with her—she fights back."

"Pay no attention to him," she said in a throaty laugh. "He's always envied Jim Bridger for being the best liar in the mountains and keeps using me for his bait when he makes up his stories. Here, give me that list," she said, grabbing the piece of paper from my hand, "and I'll give you a tour of the store." With that, she took Dennison by the arm and led him off toward the aisles and back shelves.

Not that it surprised me, for Kate was a bold woman who was used to having her way, and she got it more from straightforward talk than any currying I had ever seen. In fact, I could only remember a couple of occasions that even came close to that, and they made me feel uncomfortable.

But I couldn't help liking her. I did not see how anyone could help not liking her, especially when I stood there watching her move about the store. She was of average height and had blue eyes and bright red hair and a face that had somehow weathered the land and time. I never did ask, but I figured she was closing in on forty. She had a few wrinkles in her brow, but they were nothing like the leather that passed for the skin of my face. When I thought of it, the rest of her figure was the same as it must have been when she first got full grown, and it was nothing you would ever hear a man complain about. In the time I had known her I had never seen her wear a dress. Yet, even in Levi's and a man's work shirt, she managed to give a man the feeling that civilization was there or close by. But then, whenever a woman came to town to stay, it was a sure sign that civilization was coming for it was never long after that churches and schools started to spring up.

I took in her features one more time as she walked off, lording over the tall, lean young man whose arm she held. And I found myself feeling different about her. There was something gnawing at the back of my mind that made me feel something different about this woman at that moment. The trouble was I did not know what the feeling was or what made me feel that way. I was still thinking on it when she returned to the counter, a mischievous look about her.

"He says he escorted a girl out here," she said. When I did not reply, she said, "And from the way he talks, I'd say he's taken a shine to her." I could have turned to stone, the way I was feeling. All I knew was my neck was getting red and working its way up, and Kate's smile was getting wider, for we both knew what she was leading to. "I told him to bring her in next Sunday and the four of us will go for a ride and have a picnic. I'll fry some chicken and—"

"No," I blurted out.

"And why not?" Her smile was turning into a stubborn frown.

"Roundup," I said, avoiding her eyes. "Spring roundups coming and I gotta get everything ready. We ain't gonna have no time for picnics."

"Dallas, that's a lie and you know it! You have everything ready even when there's only you to do it, and now you have this young boy to help you, so there's no excuse.

"Oh, you old reprobate, you're still fighting me, aren't you?"

But before I could answer, she took my face in both hands and was kissing me. I pulled away as quick as I could.

"Kate! Not here, not in public!" I knew my face was blood red now.

Then she was kissing me again, only this time I did not pull back all that fast. Instead, I felt her put both arms around as much of me as she could and felt me doing the same to her. It couldn't have been all that long, but I'll be damned if I know where that kid come from.

"Ahem," I heard him mumble. "I'd hate to interrupt anything, but—"

I pulled away from her real quick, feeling like someone had planted a beet on my shoulders.

"Never argue with her," I said, looking at the boy. "Can't win. No, never can win."

But Kate did not seem to mind and I thought I saw a twinkle in her eye as she looked at the boy and said, "I wish it were true."

"Well, uh, Sonny, why don't you get the supplies and I'll square it with Kate." I was feeling about as comfortable as Custer at the Little Big Horn and in all truth wished I was there with him instead of having to answer to Kate.

"Shall I plan on making chicken for Sunday?" She said it with a lighter tone in her voice than I had heard in a long time, kind of like she was really happy.

"I don't know, Kate. I'll have to check with John," I said nervously. "We really do have a roundup coming and I'll have to see what the boss has in mind what with the way things are going."

Sometimes all you have to do is talk about trouble and it will show up. And that is exactly what happened then as Turk Calder and a couple of the ruffians who hung out with him walked into the store. Kate had her usual smile for them but I knew there was going to be trouble, especially if they started pushing the kid around again. I remembered the look on his face as he sat on the buckboard just before entering the store, and it was a vengeful one if ever I had seen one. I also knew how Kate felt about fighting inside her store, so it was going to be up to me to keep the peace one way or another.

"Good morning, gentlemen," she said. "What can I do for you?"

"Cartridges. Make 'em .44-40's." It was Turk who spoke and from the way he talked and acted, he was just coming off a night-long hoot or had started his drinking early at Ike Stockton's next door. Whatever it was, it made him do a lot of squinting. His partners were in a bit better shape.

"Here you are, Mr. Calder," Kate said, putting a box of .40-40 cartridges on the counter. "That'll be—"

"Put it on the account." Turk said it cold and mean.

"Account? I'm afraid you don't have an account with this store, Mr. Calder."

"Dolan's. His account."

It was getting hard for Kate to stretch her hospitality, what with Calder continuing to talk at a near yell.

"There's no need to raise your voice, Mr. Calder," Kate said, the smile suddenly gone. "And as for Mr. Dolan, he neither desires nor needs an account with this store, so if you'll just pay me for your purchase—"

"Like hell!" he said in the same loud voice, a sneer on his face as he picked up the box of shells.

"Shut up and pay her or get out!"

I had been keeping an eye on Turk's friends while the whole exchange was going on. He was predictable enough, but I hadn't seen these two gunnies before and if they ran with Turk they came from the same cloth. So hearing Dennison's voice behind me scared me at first because I had forgotten about him. I heard him set down the box of supplies on the counter and step out to my side to face the three.

Calder did his best to uncross his eyes, finally recognizing Sonny as the youngster he had beaten the day before. "You again!" he yelled, and this time there was outrage in his voice.

"I'll have no fighting in this store," Kate said, throwing as much authority into her voice as she could.

"Now, wait a minute," I said, holding up my hands. "Just hold on a second." I kept thinking that I had to keep peace in the store, but at the same time my mind was telling my brain how much I really hated Turk Calder. Making decisions can be awful tough sometimes. The boy was itching for a fight. All I had to do was glance at the way he kept balling up his fists. Like I said, he was not too bright, but he was showing signs of having sand.

"Now, folks," I began, "I'm thinking we ought to be able to talk this out."

"You're getting in the way again, Dallas," Turk said, mean as ever. "One of these days you're gonna wind up fighting about it."

"Just you hold on, Turk," I replied, putting a hand on his chest as he made a move forward. "Kate don't want her place busted up and that's understandable." I turned to Kate, gave her a nod of assurance and said, "I'll take care of this." Then I turned to Dennison, who was still balling his fists and ready to go at it root hog or die. "Now, Sonny, you're forgetting what I told you this morning."

"What?" the boy asked, still staring at Calder.

"I told you that they had an old saying out here, remember? 'Only a fool argues with a skunk, a mule or a cook,' it says." Out of the corner of my eye I could see one of the others edging a hand toward his gun and between that and thinking of how Turk had yelled at Kate, I couldn't help what I said next. "Of course, it don't say nothing about jackasses."

That's when I hit Turk. Square in the eye just when it had some fire coming to it. I may be small, but you tend to work up some strength hauling all of those pots and pans and beef sides around when you cook and I hit him hard enough to throw him off balance into the other two.

Sonny lit right into the one on the right, tackling him about the waist and bringing him down on top of some kind of display. I kicked the other fellow just under his knee cap and he forgot all about drawing his gun. He made the mistake of taking hold of the countertop while he hopped around on one foot, for that was when Kate brought the side of that iron skillet down on his fingers. Then he was hopping on one foot and holding both hands and letting everyone know what pain he was in. And that's when Kate brought the flat of the skillet to the front side of his face and bloodied him good as red liquid began to spurt from his nose and he sagged to the floor.

Meanwhile, I was hitting Turk as hard as I could with

both hands to the face. He was pretty well drunk, but he was as strong as a bull and it didn't make it any easier to knock him down. He was bleeding from his face and his nose and eye, but he wouldn't go down. He simply stood there like an old oak tree refusing to fall. I looked down at the blood on my knuckles, not sure if it was mine or his.

Then I felt my side cave in. It didn't come from Turk because he was still standing there. It came from the right and all of a sudden I knew the Dennison kid wasn't faring so well. I gave out a moan and he hit me in the face, knocking me back toward the counter, this third ruffian. He wasn't as big as Turk, but he was thick in the chest and about forty pounds heavier than me. I shook my head, regaining my focus, and he swung again. I ducked and hit him low. When he doubled over I brought a knee up to meet his face, but wasn't sure who got hurt the most, for my side was aching when I made that move. He fell to the floor, unconscious.

Sonny was getting up off the floor at the same time I saw Turk start to slowly move toward me. The kid must have seen it too because the next thing I saw was Sonny quickly moving around in front of the big man. Turk had a glaze to his eyes, not really seeing anything as he moved. Dennison hit him three times, a hard right, a left and an uppercut that finally knocked Turk Calder to the floor.

"Are you all right, Dallas?" Kate had come around the counter and was feeling my side as I watched Sonny, a trickle of blood coming from his mouth, slowly massage his fists as he stepped over the fallen bodies.

"Nothing liniment won't cure," I said, flinching at her probe. "How about you?" I didn't know why, but I found myself putting an arm around her waist and giving her a short hug without thinking about it.

"I'm awful sorry about breaking your table up, Missus Rogers. I'll pay you for it as soon as I can," the boy said.

"Horse apples," I said, slowly kneeling down beside the

man Sonny had taken on. I reached in his shirt pocket, pulled out some bills, gave the denomination a glance and handed them to Kate.

"But isn't that stealing?" Dennison asked suspiciously.

"You might call it the law of the land, Sonny. Out here you break it and you pay for it."

"But it was the one that knocked him down—"

"Don't matter," I said. "You may have hit him, but he's the one broke it. Besides, the wad he's got in his pocket he can afford it."

"Actually," Kate said, "you're the one who started this, Dallas. After all, you said you were going to take care of it, and look what happened."

She was making me feel uncomfortable again with her logic.

"I tried keeping the peace, Kate, honest. You heard me. I talked to both of 'em. But . . ."

"But," she repeated, waiting for an explanation.

"But I got to thinking about how he treated you, and . . ."

"And . . ."

"Well, hell," I said, grudgingly. "I've been wanting to do that for a long time."

Kate broke out in her best raucous laugh, gave me a hug before realizing that my side was hurt and looked up into my face. "Dallas Haywood, you're impossible." Then, in a lower, more intimate voice, "But I love you anyway."

"Gee, Dallas, is your side hurting that much?" Sonny asked. When I frowned at him, he added, "Well, you're turning all red. I just thought—"

That was when we heard the shots out in the street.

CHAPTER FOUR

Kate was the first one to reach the door, Sonny not far behind her. It took me a little longer, the pain in my side reminding me of how the kid must have felt the day before.

"Well, what's going on?" I demanded impatiently, half-way to the door.

"I don't know," Sonny said, "but there's two men out in that street that've been shot."

The firing, which had been poured out at a fast, even pace at first, was dying down and I could hear horses gal-loping down the street, thought I counted four quickly pass by the Montano store. They were heading east, probably toward Stinking Springs where the Kid headquartered, and were right on the edge of town when one last rifle shot rang out and one of the riders slumped forward in the saddle.

"It's Billy," Kate said, and I turned my attention to the street where the shooting occurred. Sure enough, there was Billy the Kid making his way toward the store. He was trying to run but accomplishing nothing more than a fast hobble. The inside of his pants leg was bloodied where he had been hit in the thigh. Sonny just stood there, mouth agape, as the Kid approached the storefront.

"Believe it or not, some of us survive getting shot out here," I said, but the sarcasm did not seem to penetrate the awe Sonny felt for the wounded man.

"How bad is it?" Kate asked, assisting the Kid to the counter.

"Nothing, Miss Kate," he said. "But it sure does have a

sting to it." If he was in much pain, he did a good job of not showing it and it impressed Sonny.

It was not until I near stumbled on one of the unconscious bodies that I remembered they were there. One thing I knew for sure, and that was that Brady's men would be scouring the street. I did not want Turk Calder or his henchmen aware that the young gunman was in their presence, so the Kid had to get out of there fast.

"Kate, you still got your water bucket out back?" I asked.

"Of course. Why?"

"Sonny, you quit gawking and go with Kate. Throw some water on these yahoos and get 'em the hell outta here. I'm gonna take the Kid back to your storage shed," I said to Kate. "I'll see if I can patch him up some."

Kate reached behind the counter and produced a six-gun, which she stuck in her waistband, more, I suspicioned, to impress Turk and his boys when they came to than anything else. I chuckled to myself as she did so, received a questioning look in return.

"I wonder how he's gonna take it when he finds out you can shoot better'n he can," I said in explanation, knowing the boy would ask why she had the gun on her. A lot of Easterners found it hard to believe that, contrary to what they read in the dime novels, women had to be as tough as men in this country. Part of that included knowing which end of a gun the bullet came out of, and there were a number of women who could shoot as good as any man. Kate Rogers was one of them.

While they were taking care of Calder and his men, I helped the Kid back to the storage shed and sat him on the bunk Kate loaned out occasionally to anyone staying overnight. The shed was one of those few buildings constructed of wood with a wooden floor built off the ground to keep the boxes of supplies from rotting when the rains came.

"What happened out there?" I asked, going through a pantry shelf, looking for medicines.

"Reckon I just got tired of being pushed." He said it in an even tone of voice and I could believe him. This young lad was gaining a reputation for being a bad man to tangle with and I couldn't fault the reasons for it. From what I had seen and heard of him, he liked the ladies and he liked the cards and he was damn good with a gun. Not fast, you understand, but good, and most times it was accuracy that counted as much or more than being quick on the draw. We treasured our freedom in this land and there were few men who would admit they could put up with being pushed around. The way things were going for the Kid, he had only one choice. He pushed back. Real hard.

He and the four men I saw riding off after the shooting had spent the previous night at Tunstall's store going over the wrongdoings of Dolan and his crowd and the jeopardy it had put them all in. The Kid never said whether or not they were looking down the neck of a bottle while that discussion was going on, but even if they were they came away from it in better shape than Turk and his boys. It was eventually decided that something had to be done about it. The five of them had worked up enough hate between them to wait for Brady and George Hindman, his deputy, who was no better than the sheriff.

When Brady, Hindman and three other henchmen passed the Tunstall store early in the morning, the Kid set up an ambush of his own. They figured that since Tunstall had been done in that way, Brady deserved no better. So they set up behind some adobe walls next to the Tunstall store and when Brady and his compadres left the courthouse a while later, they commenced to blow the living hell out of them. Brady and his deputy were the first ones shot and maybe the only ones, according to the Kid, because the others scattered and returned fire. That he could tell, the sheriff was dead by the time he hit the ground and Hindman was close to it, his body riddled with bullets.

"Then how'd you get this?" I asked, putting the finishing

touches on a makeshift bandage I had tied around his thigh. The Kid now sat on the bunk with only his long johns on as he continued his story.

"Well, the shooting died down and we figured the others had took off, so the boys got the horses and I went after this." He held up the Winchester repeater that hadn't left his grasp since he entered the store. "Brady took it from me when he arrested me back in February for the Tunstall killing, then refused to return it to me when he let me and Fred go." A crooked grin crossed his face, accompanied by a look of satisfaction as he stared at the weapon. "But I got it back. By God, I did."

"That when you got hit?"

"Yeah. I went out to Brady's body to get my rifle and took a slug. The boys had already mounted, so they took off and there I was, alone."

"So you hightailed it over here, knowing Kate'd take you in." Whether what he'd done was right or wrong, I wasn't too awful happy about what I knew would follow.

"She's a good woman, cookie," he said with a smile. "Kind of grows on you after a while, if you know what I mean."

"Coming here just brought trouble, Kid," I said, starting to feel defensive about his presence. "Dolan finds out you're here and this place is gonna turn into a regular graveyard. So you just remember one thing," I said, jabbing a finger at him. "I'll patch you up, but don't look for any help when they come after you. I ain't no gunfighter."

"And I ain't asking for your help, friend." The smile was gone, replaced by a serious look and a tone of voice that held more than just a little defiance. He was a tough bird, this Billy the Kid, and he wouldn't have anyone else fighting his battles for him. That was plain to see. In that same moment, in that same look, I could see why this youngster moved in only certain areas. For all of the toughness in his voice, in his look, whether real or simply a front, Billy the

Kid was a loner, and at that particular time and place it was
the animal look of survival that was evident in him. Like a
pup that had been wounded, he would never let anyone
get that close to him again, never fully trust another person.

Kate and Sonny came in then, a look of urgency on both
their faces.

"What's the matter?" I said, "you have trouble getting
rid of Calder and his toughs?"

"No, no," Kate said. "I just held a gun on them while
Sonny brought them to. I think they were all in too much
pain to want to start anything again."

"Then what's wrong?"

"It's Dolan's men. When we got Calder out the front
door, Sonny spotted Dolan raising a mob of his so-called
deputies. I'll wager money they're going to search each
and every store and house until they find him," she said,
looking at the Kid.

"See what I mean," I said, giving the Kid a cold frown.

"What's going on?" Kate asked, seeing the disapproval
on my face.

"Never mind," I said. "You two get him the hell out of
here. I don't care how, but if you don't want any more
blood spilled in your store, Kate, you'll do it." Then, to
Sonny, "Whatever she says, you do. Understand?"

"Sure," he said. "But where are you going?"

"I'm gonna load them supplies on the wagon and see can
I keep Dolan's crowd out of back here."

Then Kate was by my side again.

"Are you all right? Maybe Sonny should go."

"Don't you worry 'bout me, woman," I said, finding room
for a smile, even in all of the chaos. " 'Tain't the first time
my sides been stove up."

It was true that I'd been bruised in the ribs before, even
had a couple of them broken, but the experience never did
feel any easier with each passing. I found that out when I

carried the box of supplies out to the buckboard. The pain was deeper than I'd ever felt before and I would've dropped the box, light as it was, if I had to walk any further than I did. It was then I saw a dozen or so of Dolan's deputies approaching the store. I walked back in the store, trying to act as though I didn't see them, but they weren't going to bypass the Montano store.

"Where's the Rogers woman?" one demanded when they barged in.

"Out back, I reckon. She had to get something from the back, as I recall." It was hard to sound disinterested when I knew as well as they did just what they were looking for.

"What's this doing here?" another asked, noticing the blood on the floor. "You haven't seen that Bonney kid have you?"

I never was much for lying, so I just hedged the truth some. "Next time you see Turk Calder, you ask him where he spent his time last time he was in Montano's store and if he don't say it was flat on his back, you tell him I said he's a liar." I leaned up against the counter, winced when the edge prodded my side. "I've got some tender ribs to prove it, too," I added.

But they didn't seem to be all that interested in my tale, because the anxious one wanted to get on with business. "You ask me, boss, she's been gone long enough. I say she's hiding the Kid."

"You're probably right," the leader said, and proceeded on back through the rear entrance.

If I had my shotgun, I would've stopped them right then and there, not to help the Kid, but for Kate's sake. As it was they pushed on past me and I was bringing up the rear as I watched them enter the storage shed. All of us were ready for a massacre, but not a shot was fired as the first three entered the small building with guns drawn. It surprised me as well as them and I found myself pushing bodies aside as I made my way inside.

The leader was standing in front of Kate, gun in hand, while his two cronies were searching behind every box they could see, looking for Billy the Kid. But he was nowhere to be found. The only people in the shed were Kate and Sonny, she attending to his side while he sat on the bunk.

"I thought you said she was getting something," the man said suspiciously.

"Well, she—"

"He's obviously mistaken," Kate said. "As you can see, I'm fixing up this young man's side. In case Mr. Haywood didn't tell you, sir, there was a fight in my store just a short time ago. Mr. Haywood and his friend gave Turk Calder a sound thrashing."

"He came this way, boss. I tell you, I saw him coming toward this store."

"Then I'm afraid you truly are mistaken. Perhaps you saw him enter Mr. Stockton's saloon. It's right next door, you know. But as you can see, he's not on my premises."

None of them were happy about not finding the Kid, especially the leader, whose face turned an ugly shade of red. "Lady, if you're lying to me, you're gonna regret it. I swear you will."

I never did take to revolvers, leaning more toward that scattergun of mine for any shooting arguments. But all of those years in the mountains had gotten me used to carrying a bowie knife and I took my time pulling it out now.

"Mister, did I ever tell you 'bout them vigilantes I seen down in Texas oncet?"

"Vigilantes?" He cocked a suspicious eye at me.

"Well," I started out real calm, "they hung this man for something or other, I forget which. And you know, one of them fellas was right mean. Yes, sir, meaner'n a rattlesnake in a skillet." I paused. "Yup. You see, friend, he skinned that fella they hung. I mean he skinned him front and back! Made a pair of moccasins for hisself, as I recall." It wasn't a

tale for the squeamish and I thought I almost saw the ruffian I was speaking to wince at one point.

"So what?"

"Well, son," I said, playing with the point of the knife, "if
I hear you make one more threat to Mrs. Rogers like that,
or if you even come close to touching her, well"—and here
I grinned, just mischievously enough to let him know I was
serious—"I reckon I'll fit me for a new pair of moccasins. In
fact, if you ain't outta here in about thirty seconds, I may do
it right now."

There was no doubt that my knife was little or no match
for the firepower of these toughs and for a second I thought
he didn't believe me. His hand was moving toward the
holstered Colt revolver and I was getting ready to count
my chips before I cashed them in, when I heard the cocking of another six-gun to my side.

"I think you'd better take his advice, mister," Sonny said,
leveling Kate's .44 right at this fellow's brisket. Whether
the man thought the boy could use the weapon in his hand
made little difference, for there were only a dozen or so
feet between the two and at that range all Sonny had to do
was pull the trigger.

"I'm gonna remember you, kid," the man said with a
deadly vehemence in his voice.

Dennison only shrugged, smiled briefly. "I didn't catch
your name."

"Shatten," the big man said.

"I'll keep it in mind. My friends call me Sonny," he said,
still smiling. "But it'll be a cold day in hell before I call you
friend."

Sonny waved the gun barrel toward the entrance and
the crowd began leaving. It was when they had left that I
realized that I was as stunned at Sonny's actions as Dolan's
men must have been. He looked and acted the part of a
tenderfoot and no one would take him seriously, at least
before this morning no one would have. But being in a fist

fight and then backing down part of the Dolan gang was sure to give him some credibility once the word got out. And it always did.

"That took a lot of guts, kid."

"Yeah, I guess," he said. Then he looked down at the shaking gun in his fist, comprehending what he'd just done. "Do you always feel this way?"

"Only if you're human, Sonny," Kate said, giving him a gentle pat on the arm. "You did fine. I'm proud of you."

"By the way, where is the Kid? Billy, I mean." I'd nearly forgotten the reason for the intrusion and was as curious as the others as to where the young gunman could have disappeared to.

"Oh, he was here all the time," Kate said with a smile, bending down on the far side of the bunk and lifting up part of the floor underneath the bunk. The piece of flooring was about the size of a coffin lid and was apparently a cover for a hollowed-out bottom beneath it. And slowly, climbing out of it, was Billy the Kid.

CHAPTER FIVE

"Well, I'll be damned," was all I could whisper in as low a voice as astonishment will take. That may be the only time that me and the pilgrim had the same expression on our faces at the same time.

"Most of us are," Billy said, slowly working his way out of the coffin-like area he'd been in. He'd wince when the pain in his leg got to him, but for the most part he was smiling when he said it. Not that I blamed him. Hell, if he'd so much as sneezed, he'd likely have gotten one hell of a case of lead poisoning that leads to a permanent case of death. And knowing Dolan's bunch, they'd leave him right where he lay for a coffin. Me, I purely hate to clean up a mess like that, so I just grumbled.

"Gee, Mr. Bonney," Sonny was saying with awe, "that was—"

"Stupid," I said, finishing the sentence for him. From the look on Sonny's face, the boy had a new hero to look up to, one I wasn't all too sure was the right kind. Let's just say I'd have felt a sight better about it if it was John Chisum the boy was looking up to instead of Billy the Kid.

"Oh, I don't know," Kate said looking at the Kid and Sonny with that contagious smile of hers, "I thought it was kind of heroic."

"Don't pay no never mind to her, boy. You're a *cook*, not a gunman." I still had the bowie in my hand and found myself shaking it at him the way a mother does a warning finger. For some reason, Kate found that humorous and began to put some mischief into that smile of hers while I

spoke. "Well, it's true!" I said defensively, now talking to
the woman I hadn't long ago kissed. "What happened right
here is an occupational hazard to Billy, not some kind of
heroism." I spit the word out the way you do the first taste
you get of your mama's lye soap. "Only thing the boy here's
gonna sling is hash, and he don't even know how to do that
yet!"

"Oh, Dallas." Some things Kate never could see my point
of view on and this was one of them, as she dismissed my
speechifying. And that didn't make me feel any easier
about it.

"You got any smarts," I said to Billy, who seemed to be
enjoying it all, "you'll light a shuck afore those birds decide
to come back for a second look."

"Sure thing," the young gunman said, not the least bit
ruffled by what I'd said. As he readied to leave, he added,
"Thanks, Kate, I owe you one."

Then he was gone.

I all but herded young Dennison back to the store to load
what was left of the supplies we'd originally come for, but
not even that got done on time.

"Dallas, come quick!" Kate said, sticking her head out
the back door not five minutes later. Like I say, this woman
doesn't rattle easy, so when she says come quick, you come
quick. Today I was going as quick as my side would allow
and Dennison beat me to it getting back inside.

"Well, looks like Dallas was right," I heard a familiar
voice say as I slowly made my way into the Montano store.
When I got through the back entrance, there was Uncle
John, bigger than life. "You youngsters heal in no time," he
said with a smile. Then, glancing at me, his face dead serious, he added, "Or was that Dallas chasing you?" Chisum
had a sense of humor that could be about as dry as a mirage
full of water at high noon in the desert at times, and if you
didn't know him or what he was talking about, why, you'd
never catch on.

" 'Course not," I said, with just as straight a face, "ain't got my cleaver." The corners of his eyes wrinkled just a mite to let me know he still remembered, and there was a moment of silence before he spoke.

"You heard about Sheriff Brady and Hindman being killed, I presume."

"I guess he was right about—" Dennison began, but I nudged his side, the one that hurt him, and he shut up.

"Yeah, boss, heard the shots and all," I said casually. My new assistant must have caught on to what I'd intended for all he gave me was a silent, wrinkled brow. Kid might have some brains after all. "By the way, what are you doing in town?"

"I rode in with Mr. McSween this morning. We had some business to take care of." Not that I distrust Uncle John, you understand, but if he didn't see the curiosity in my eye when he said that last piece . . . well, maybe we're all getting old.

"Looks like we might be here the night, Dallas," he continued. "Why don't you get a couple sacks of Arbuckles and head on over to the jail—"

"Jail!" The way he said it, you'd have thought Woodrow Dennison was about to become a permanent fixture in the Lincoln County hoosegow.

"That's what I said, son. You and Dallas get on over there and take a decent-sized coffeepot and I'll be along directly." Then, turning his attention to Kate, he said, "I've got to pay Miss Rogers for some of our supplies." He did it every time I was around her, calling Kate *Miss* Rogers when everyone knew she'd been widowed for some time now. And Kate responded to it every time with a blush, just as she was doing now. Maybe John Chisum was playing matchmaker, but all I ever got was the urge to get out of the presence of those two when he said what he did. It was enough to make a man wish he was fighting the Apaches, as surrounded as you got to feeling. So I picked out a brand-new coffeepot from Kate's stock and me and Dennison headed for the jail. Slowly.

"What did you mean back there about not having the cleaver?" the lad asked as soon as we'd left the store.

"Damn, but you're a curious creature," I said, feeling more like a baby-sitter than the boss to an assistant cook. These pilgrims are just full of questions when they get out here, but not a one of them has got the patience to wait until after the day's work's been done to do their jawing. No, sir. Still, the story behind my remark to Uncle John was an amusing one, so I told him about it. What the hell, we had a ways to walk and we weren't going to get there any faster at the laggardly pace we were going.

"Well, son, the way I figure it you earn everything you get in life, good, bad or indifferent," I began. "Trouble is some folks don't figure they have to earn anything, and Santos was one of 'em." I chuckled, remembering the incident. "Big border ruffian from down Mexico way.

"He was lolling around the bunkhouse one day, so I told him to go out and get me a steer to slaughter. Boys come back early that afternoon and got right riled at me just a-sitting there not having more than coffee to offer 'em. Man works hard, he expects a decent meal toward the end of the day. I told 'em 'bout Santos not delivering the steer I'd asked for and they took off for the bunkhouse. Next thing you know there's Santos charging through the door to my cookshack like he owned the goddamn place, and madder'n hell to boot!

" 'Who you think you are, getting the outfit mad at me? I don't take orders from no cook!' he shouted at me. By that time the boys had blocked the doorway to see what would happen. That's when I picked up my cleaver and told the sorry ass I was the man who was gonna serve him up for supper, apple stuck in his mouth and all, ary he didn't come up with the goods right quick."

"Well, what happened?" the lad said after I paused for a moment.

"Why, I took off after Santos, of course! I may be a bandy-legged little rooster, but I wasn't carrying around all that extra weight that Santos was either. Chased him around the bunkhouse twicet, I think it was. Had him out in the open then and he taken off for the main house. Run up that veranda and was heading for the front door when Uncle John was coming out and everything just sort of come to a halt. When he found out, Chisum set Santos straight 'bout the cookshack and who runs what and I had me the beef straight away. Yes, sir."

The boy's grin had widened as I told the story and he broke out into laughter toward the end of it. But after a short silence a serious look came to his face.

"Dallas, you wouldn't really have—"

I stopped short and looked him straight in the eye.

"You can take it to the bank, son."

"But that's . . . I mean, this Santos character—"

"Santos was wild boar hog, Sonny, and I'd have skewered him in a minute," I said with conviction. I never had taken after the Donners or the Alfred Packers of the frontier and likely wouldn't have done it, but making believers out of those who questioned me and my domain never did hurt. "On the other hand, I ain't had any complaints about requests I've made of the boys since then either."

"What about Santos? What happened to him?"

"Didn't last two weeks. I told Uncle John he ate twice as much as the others about the same time Tom Lang told him he did half the work of any other man in the outfit. You gotta raise more sweat than on your upper lip if you're gonna last on the Jinglebob. Guaranteed."

I was hoping that the lad would get the idea that loafers and loudmouths like Turk Calder and Santos never did find a permanent place in this land. If I could get him to realize that then I would only have to worry about what I was sure would be a budding interest in the way of life of Billy the Kid. Not that I didn't sometimes like the Kid my own self, you understand. It's just that any man who becomes a legend in his own time generally don't live too long out here, especially if his reputation is made with a gun.

We walked the rest of the way in silence, but once we got to the jail I still wasn't too awful sure what was going on. The building itself was a small one, but for all the horses surrounding it, why, you'd have thought they were having a convention or something. Neither Dennison or I got too warm a welcome when we asked questions about what was going on, so we waited for Uncle John to show up and explain things.

"Dennison, you find some deadwood and get a fire going and make us some coffee," Chisum said right off when he arrived. Then, glancing at me, he said, "He does know how to make coffee, doesn't he, Dallas?"

"At least," I said, and nodded to the boy to do as he'd been told. Then I followed Uncle John into the jail.

"They're gone," were the first words I heard inside the jail. Not distressed as much as concerned was how they sounded. They came from a man I'd come to know only as Dr. Leverson. He was what Dennison, being an Easterner, would likely call distinguished, at least from the way he dressed. He'd come from Colorado and was staying with Chisum as he scouted the Pecos Valley for what might be a decent place to bring some settlers he was associated with. Not that I had much to do with him, but the few times I'd heard him speak I'd gotten the idea he knew more words than Webster and had memorized at least three different encyclopedias. But he never looked down his nose at you, and in comparison to most pilgrims who flaunted their education he was an odd bird out here.

"Where to?" was John's reply.

"The Army has removed them to Fort Stockton for protection," Leverson said, "or so they say."

"I should've figured it." It was a grumble more than the expected chuckle that came from Uncle John this time, and it wasn't a time to tangle with him. John Chisum didn't hold any everlasting love for the Army, at least not that which was run in the New Mexico Territory, and I couldn't blame him one bit. It wasn't long ago that he'd asked for the assistance of the Army in catching some rustlers who were cutting out bits and pieces of his herd and been denied. Like I say, the Jinglebob is a big outfit.

"Wait a minute," I said, "I'm feeling like the one fella at the necktie party that ain't heard who else was invited." Dr. Leverson gave me a strange glance, then looked at Uncle John with a frown as if Chisum'd given me a secret recipe. "Just who is THEY?"

The two men looked at one another with a mixture of false hope and the same amount of expectation, making it obvious that both thought the other had filled me in but hadn't.

"You know, some years back I resolved that I'd never believe a body that told me about 'they,' " I said to the two men, who must, by now, have felt a bit embarrassed. "Young lad I was working with down in the panhandle a number of years back took the boys out to do some scouting while I tended to a wound I'd gotten. He come riding back over the horizon like a swarm of bees was after him. 'They're coming! They're coming!' he yells out from a distance. I didn't make no never mind 'bout it cause I figured he was talking 'bout the rest of the party." Here I paused long enough to cock a deceptive eye toward Uncle John and the good doctor before saying, "*They* turned out to be half the Comanche nation!"

"Really?" I looked behind me to see Dennison standing there in the doorway. "Did you make it out alive?"

"Why, a carse I did, pilgrim! I'm the one telling the story, ain't I?" Then, turning back to Chisum and the good doctor, I said, "But I still ain't found out who THEY are this time."

They, as it turned out, were McSween and three of his hands. It seems that after Brady and Hindman got shot there were more than just those plug uglies who'd come to the Montano store looking for Billy the Kid who were turning things upside down. All of a sudden there was some fellow who thought he was a "special" appointee of the court and he, along with some troops who were right handy at the moment, took a notion to put McSween and his men under arrest for the killing of Brady and Hindman. The whole thing seemed impossible to believe because John Chisum had ridden in with McSween and his men, and I knew the big rancher better than that. Chisum wouldn't have authorized any such killing as had taken place this morning.

"There's more than just the Murphy-Dolan outfit involved here," Uncle John said to no one in particular.

"I thought everyone already knew that," I said.

"Then, sir, perhaps I could be of some help," Leverson said. "I could write a letter or two to some acquaintances I have . . ." The sentence trailed off and I got the same feeling I always do about these civilized birds from back East. They talk a good game but they'd lose their shirt if they played bunkhouse poker.

"And who's that gonna be," I snorted, losing some of my liking for Leverson, "one of them fancy lawyers from Denver?" I was shaking my head in disbelief but it didn't ruffle his feathers any.

"Actually, I was thinking of writing someone who could *do* something about the situation," he said calmly.

"See?" I gave Uncle John a knowing glance, then threw a more disgusted one over my shoulder at Dennison and added, "Pilgrims."

"Actually, I was thinking about writing Carl Schurz, and, of course, Rutherford." Still calm as could be.

"Is this what you called me over for, John?" I asked, a bit perturbed at what was going on. "To make coffee for some pilgrim who's gonna write a couple of no-accounts?"

This time it was Chisum who was shaking his head in disbelief, and I'd swear I saw the kid start to grin out of the corner of my eye.

"Dallas," John said, "Mr. Schurz is the Secretary of the Interior, and Rutherford . . . well, I believe his last name is Hayes. You remember him, don't you? He's the man they address as Mr. President back East."

"Oh." I don't think I ever said anything softer or with more surprise in my life. But you can bet I wasn't about to stand around and let these people see if the rest of me was going to turn as red as my face just then. "Well, then, Doc, you just set to and do your writing," I boomed in as loud and friendly a voice as I could muster. "Long as you got ink in the well, I'll put coffee in your cup." Then I shooed Dennison out of there just so I had a reason to get out my own self. Fact is, I was wishing those Comanches were around so I could take out my anger on them.

My young assistant was catching on quick and knew better than to chide me or even talk to me as we worked our way back around to the fire and coffee. But it wasn't five minutes later that Uncle John came striding around the side of the jail, a none too happy look about him. The Dennison boy was standing just a couple of feet away from me and when Uncle John spoke, it was the youngster he was addressing all right. But it was me he was staring at all the time.

"There's something you might want to remember, Mr. Dennison, especially out here. Never *assume*. It makes an *ass* out of *you* and *me*." He paused a moment, the tension building that short distance there was between us. It's that sort of time that makes the difference whether you walk away from a Mexican standoff or go root hog or die. Only with John and me it was friendship more than a life and death matter that was being tested now.

"How about if I get some coffee for you two," Dennison said. Like I say, the boy was catching on fast. But from the look in Chisum's eye I got the idea that he didn't know or care at the moment that the boy was present.

"I expected better from you, Dallas," was all Uncle John said before leaving. I couldn't remember a time when John Chisum and I hadn't been able to talk out any differences we might have had.

But watching him walk away like that I was beginning to wonder.

CHAPTER SIX

One pot of coffee was all that was needed that afternoon as Leverson set to writing his letters. He and Uncle John spent a good deal of time talking that afternoon and by late afternoon we had pulled up stakes and headed back to the Jinglebob. Chisum had been less than cordial in giving orders that afternoon, which likely accounts for the grumbling I did when Kate showed up shortly before we left.

"I'm gonna fry up that chicken Sunday morning, Dallas, so you be sure to bring Sonny and that new girl with you, understand?" she said, taking hold of my arm in what I reckon she figured to be a romantic fashion of sorts.

"I'll see, Kate, I'll see."

"My, but aren't we impatient today." Kate could be a mite scornful when she wanted to and it was a side of her I didn't like, but then, I reckon no man does. On the other hand, I wasn't in much of a mood for it right then, be it Chisum or Kate.

"Look," I said harshly, turning on her with as mean a look as I'd ever remembered giving Turk Calder, "this ain't been one of my best days, so if I was you, woman, I'd back off a good bit. *We* are impatient today, yes. You can bet your—"

"Say, Dallas, where do you want—" the Dennison boy began before seeing what was taking place. "Oh . . . uh, sorry, folks, I was . . . look, I didn't mean to—"

"Nonsense, Mr. Dennison." The smile was back on Kate's face but I'd bet all the gold in the Superstitions that I was the only one who could see the fire in her eyes. Totally ignoring me, she addressed the boy. "I'm going to have more fried chicken than I know what to do with this coming Sunday, Sonny, and I'd like to have you as my guest if you like."

The kid had tangle foot of the tongue again, taken completely by surprise.

"Close your mouth 'fore it hits your belt buckle," I said, still mad. But no one seemed to hear me.

"Yes, ma'am," Dennison gulped eagerly.

"There are just two stipulations," Kate said.

"You just name 'em, ma'am, and I'll do whatever I can to make sure they get carried out!" From the look of him, the boy could already taste Kate's cooking. Fact is, I could too—I just wasn't admitting to it.

"First, you must bring your Miss Dawson. I'd very much like to meet her." Just as Dennison had regained what he likely called composure, Kate had said something that nearly made him swallow his tongue.

"Well, ma'am . . . if she'll agree to it, I—"

"Of course she will." The way she said it, you'd think there was nothing to it.

"If you say so, ma'am."

"Secondly"—here she gave me a hard glance—"don't bring Mr. Haywood along unless you can teach him some manners." That last she said with a quick, mischievous smile, knowing what my reaction would be. I gave a quick, surprised look at the boy and took a long stride after her, only to realize that she'd sped from my sight faster than I thought she could move. I stopped, looked back at Dennison, who was now grinning like he had the upper hand.

"Don't say a thing," I growled at him, "not one damn thing. Now get this place cleaned up!"

The sound of the human voice was scarcely heard on the trip back to the ranch. Chisum seemed embroiled in his own thoughts about what had happened that day and the effect it would have on the not too distant future. Dennison had that innocent, pleased look we all had at his age, thinking about some girl somewhere and what might happen. Margaret Dawson in his case. Me, I was preparing myself for all the griping I was going to hear about not getting supper on time again when we pulled into the ranch. But I hardly heard the bellyaching the hands were doing as we pulled up before the house and I saw Margaret Dawson standing there on the veranda, holding hands with Tom Lang.

I knew in an instant what was going through Dennison's mind, but by the time I slapped my hand down beside me to where he should have been . . . well, he wasn't! By the time I caught sight of him, he was halfway to the veranda. I couldn't see his eyes, but running hell for leather like that, I'd have bet the ranch they were filled with hate. The damn fool likely hadn't even thought of whether this Dawson girl would accept his invite to Kate's Sunday social. And going up against Tom Lang to boot! And not a body in that yard stopping him!

Well, that tore it!

"STOP IT!" I yelled at the top of my lungs, surprised that the loudness didn't break the glass in the windows. But the only one who responded to it was Dennison and it did him more harm than good. He was halfway up the steps when he stopped, turned to look at me, then remembered what he originally had in mind and went flying down the stairs backward as Lang hit him hard across the jawline. He must've figured that after having the last couple of swipes at Turk Calder that day he could take on the world. Now he was making a fool of himself in front of the whole outfit. And my day wasn't getting any better.

By the time he got unsprawled from the position he lay in, I was off the wagon and halfway to him. Either he didn't see me or didn't care, because he got right back up as Lang walked down the veranda steps to meet him, the grin on his face saying he was going to have some fun. The Dawson girl, well, she had a panicky look about her as she backed off, stopped only by the wall behind her, bringing her hands up to her mouth just like you'd read in those worth-less dime novels.

Now, Tom Lang is a big man, so seeing him effortlessly block a swing the boy took at him and then knock him flat on his keister didn't surprise anyone, least of all Lang. And that's when I had my chance. He had his eyes trained on Dennison, who was rubbing his jaw for the second time and seriously giving thought as to whether or not to get back up again.

"Tom," I said, casual as could be, still walking toward him. By the time he looked up to say "Yeah," I was close enough to hit him, and I did. Across the same jawline he'd hit Sonny. It staggered him, surprised him, which was all I wanted. Before he could get a fist in action, I had one of my hands on his shoulder while the other rammed into his face several times like one of those fancy jack hammers the miners use. That staggered him some more and I stepped inside real quick like and kicked a foot out from under him. Now, I won't say that the ground settled when he fell, but everyone in that outfit knew it when Tom Lang bit the dust. He was shaking his head, getting his senses back as I stepped inside his legs and rammed a foot up against his elsewheres. It'd been a long time since I'd fought anyone in front of the crew and Tom Lang hadn't been around then, so the look on his face was decidedly one of disbelief. I took the moment to flash Lang a brief smile to let him know I was enjoying this as much as he had enjoyed hitting on Dennison.

"Been sitting on your horse too long, Tom," I said loud enough for everyone to hear. "Only thing getting hard is your butt. You carry as much deadwood or slaughtered beef and Arbuckles as I do, you might work yourself into better shape." That gave the hands a laugh, breaking the tension in some parts, but it was still there between me and

Lang. Then, in a lower voice that only the two of us knew was being spoken, I added, "You get up and do anything but walk off, friend, and I'll guarantee you that the next time you sing to the moon the wolves are gonna notice a considerable difference in your voice." I'm not sure he figured I was serious or not, but you can bet he was thinking on it real hard as I nudged my foot a bit harder against his elsewheres.

"What about Chisum?" he said, propping himself up on his elbows. "I didn't start this fandango, you know." He glared at Dennison, who was now standing upright, although a bit unsteadily.

"I didn't see Uncle John stop it, either." I took a step back, offered him a hand in getting up.

"Tom! Woodrow! Are you all right?" It was the Dawson girl running out toward us. The two combatants both flushed before giving each other looks of hatred. I think Dennison was blushing more because everyone knew his real name now than he was about the fight, and that meant he might have more fights than he could handle if he couldn't take the ribbing. As for the girl, well, she was playing it like she was in one of those fancy back East theater plays, as dramatic as she was sounding. Not doing a bad job of it either.

Except I wasn't having any of it.

"WELL, WHAT'RE YOU LOOKING AT, YOU CROSS-EYED LOAFERS!" I yelled at the top of my lungs as I faced the crew. "You want to eat, you gotta work for it! Now, one of you find me some matches and the rest of you get me some deadwood and lay these supplies in. You know where they go." They stood there befuddled for a moment, a few of them glancing back and forth at Uncle John and me, not sure who to be taking orders from. So I pulled my bowie about the same time I said "GIT!" and that settled that.

"Getting ready to take over the spread, are you, Dallas?" Chisum had dismounted, slowly approached the four of us,

Dennison, Tom Lang, the girl and me. Like I say, I wasn't in the mood to be taking any backtalk from anyone just then.

"You might run the ranch, but I run the kitchen," I said, sheathing the bowie and planting both hands on my hips. "And I'll tell you something else, *Mr.* Chisum. I feed you at the main house, you're each gonna have to take a portion off'n your plate for her, 'cause I flat ain't feeding her!"

"What!" Chisum and Lang sounded off in unison with a bit of disbelief thrown in. "And just how do you figure that?" Chisum went on, not happy about what I'd said at all.

"Sign in my kitchen applies to everyone, boss." I cocked my head to one side, looking out of the corner of my eye at him, as defiant as ever. " *'Annoying the cook will result in smaller portions','* " I said, repeating the well-known quote for his benefit. Then I shifted my gaze to Margaret Dawson as the beginnings of real fear shown in those eyes. "And I find it annoying as hell when a woman, especially a pretty one, takes to playing one man against another and one of 'em is my helper."

"Keep it up, Haywood, and you could find yourself out of a job." I was almost expecting it from Chisum, but to my surprise it came from Tom Lang. Still trying to impress the girl, I reckon.

"Oh? And who the hell's gonna do your cooking? The only thing I seen you do around here is give orders and talk mean. Hmph! You'd likely kill the whole crew in one meal!" I glanced at Chisum. "I've tasted your trail cooking. The boys'd die of malnutrition if Chisum did the cooking." To the girl I said, "I'd hate to think of what you don't know 'bout cooking.

"Come on, Sonny, we got us some people to feed." I said it walking away from the speechless trio.

Dennison stayed by my side, step for step, not once look-ing back at the woman he must've thought of only minutes before as his true love.

Like I say, the boy was catching on quick.

CHAPTER SEVEN

If ever there was a contest for who was the quietest whisperer, I'd gauge it was held at the community table that night for I didn't hear a word spoken when I fed the crew. I don't know what they were thinking, but the smart ones likely had it running through their mind that if they did open their mouth it might not see food for some time. Hunger'll do strange things to a man, if you know what I mean.

What was even more surprising was the attitude the boys had toward Dennison the next morning. Nearly all of them had heard Lang sarcastically call him Woodrow during the attempted fight. But even if they were still cautious around me when I served up flannel cakes—even then a spatula was sharp enough on its side to slit your gullet if a body took a mind to—it was a more cheerful "Hi, Sonny" and "Sonny" this and "Sonny" that when the youngster was around. The only other thing that surprised me that morning was that the boy actually showed up for work on time without me coming to get him. Either he was catching on quicker than I thought he could, or he sat up all night rubbing his jaw and thinking on that damn fool girl. And as long as he did his job, I really didn't care.

"Why are they being so friendly?" the boy asked when he'd made a trip back into the kitchen, a puzzled look about him. "I figured I wouldn't get through breakfast without some sort of a fight after what they heard last night about my name being Woodrow and all."

"Me, too." I glanced over my shoulder at the normality

things had gone back to, the cowhands jawing between mouthfuls of food. They were doing everything from joking to complaining just like always, but something had changed and I thought I knew what it was. "Appears to me it's what the boys *saw* last night more than what they heard."

"Sir?"

"Don't—"

"I know, don't call you that, you work for a living. But what do you mean by what they saw last night? It was just a fight between me and Lang," the lad shrugged, seemingly passing it off as nothing.

"It was more'n that, Sonny," I said, throwing the last of a stack of griddle cakes on a plate before handing them to the boy. "Here, get this out to 'em and take some more syrup. Won't be long afore Lang will be expecting them to be ready to ride."

He did what he was told without question and I found myself wondering if he wasn't just a mite scared of me this morning too. When he returned he grabbed the coffeepot, disappeared and returned, setting the empty one aside and preparing a new one to boil. The first thing I'd explained to him was that no self-respecting cook ever let a day go by without Arbuckles on the fire for anyone wanting it and the boy seemed to be taking my advice to heart. An extra piece of deadwood added to the fire and he was right back beside me, wanting to hear every word I had to say.

"Fact is, son, they likely figure you're grittier than fish eggs rolled in sand." He squinted at me, confused, and I added, "Brave, that's one way of saying it out here." But when the squint didn't change I knew it wasn't the definition the boy was thinking on, it was the why. So I told him.

"Tom Lang's been here a couple of years, Sonny, and he's kept a good rein on Chisum's crew. So good, in fact, that no one's ever really challenged him."

"And last night I did." Yup, he was catching on real quick.

The sun wasn't up yet but the crew was done eating, so I waited until they'd gotten through their *"Hasta la vista's"* and "See you later, Sonny" partings before I continued. Besides, I was getting tired of talking in a lower than normal voice.

"What you did last night is the equivalent of a gopher walking in on a rattlesnake convention, boy." There wasn't all that much contempt in my voice, but it didn't keep the boy from raising an eyebrow out of curiosity. "It was stupid but brave." A hurt, embarrassed look came to his face and, like any baby-sitter, I realized that the boy needed something to make him feel good about himself again. " 'Course, none of them's had the courage to go up against Tom Lang either. So even if you did get knocked ass over tea kettle, you showed 'em something they been wanting to know for two years."

"I don't understand."

"That Tom Lang's as tough as he makes himself out to be and ought not to be tangled with." That seemed to satisfy him for the moment as we set to cleaning up the community table, but it wasn't long before the boy was thinking again.

"But what about you?" he asked from across the table. "We all saw what you did to Lang. Why, he didn't even take a swing at you when he got up!"

"Oh, what I did to Lang wasn't nothing, son. But I'll tell you what. Ain't nobody on this spread got any question 'bout who runs the kitchen." Not even John Chisum, I thought to myself.

We were just about through cleaning up when Dennison paused—probably thinking again, which, so far, was his only strong suit next to being bullheaded—and gave me one of those curious looks again.

"Dallas?"

"Yeah."

"What was it you said to Lang while you had him down on the ground last night?"

"Oh, that." He'd caught me with my guard down because normally no one would have asked such a question, knowing it was none of their business in the first place. But then, this Dennison kid was a pilgrim, so maybe I should have expected it. After all, from the youngster's point of view, it was likely an innocent enough request. Now, son, what with the lack of real honest to goodness citified supplies, one of the first things you learn to do as a cook out here is to use your imagination some. And that's just what I did with Dennison. "It was nothing, really. Just a short conversation on his grandchildren."

"Really?" He had that confused look again.

"Honest."

"Gee," the boy said, walking away to another chore, talking to himself in earnest, "I didn't think he looked that old."

Tom Lang had proved himself a hard man, but I'd always known him to be a fair one when it came down to it, and if nothing else he had my respect as a man. I figured I owed him at least that much.

The crew had unloaded the supplies we'd brought back from Lincoln the night before, so it looked to be a fairly easy day to get through. Not that being a cook's an easy job, you understand, for it's likely the hardest job on a ranch, especially when it's the size of the Jinglebob. Most of those loafers who call themselves cowhands figure all a cookie's got to do is yell "Fall to" and his work's done for the day. But if any of those cowhands had any idea of how much work I do in the course of a day . . . well, they'd know why I call them loafers.

One of the chores I get saddled with each day is busting up whatever deadwood I can find so it'll fit that Ben Franklin of mine or other cooking areas. Cut it, carry it, the whole thing. The sun wasn't much past being up when I figured I'd have my newfound helper lend a hand at busting up some firewood, but from the look on his face, it wasn't something he treasured doing. Not that I could blame him either. My knuckles weren't exactly feeling agile this morning from the beating I'd given Tom Lang. Still, I'd been around a few days and my hands had been in worse shape at one time or another so I made do. Dennison didn't seem like he could handle it all that well though.

"Damn, but that hurts," he said an hour later, walking in and shaking a fist in agony. It wasn't nothing more than a blister, but the way he was acting you'd have thought he'd cut his finger off with the ax blade.

"Pilgrims," I muttered with a shake of the head, visioning one more delay in my day's work.

"I could fix it." The voice behind me almost startled me. When I turned I saw that the Little Miss Sweetness voice belonged to Margaret Dawson. But she looked different than she had the night before. Her hair was pulled back, a kerchief tying it down in place. She'd shed her fancy dresses for more practical clothes for the country she was in now, wearing a man-style shirt and jeans that fit right good. I'd seen Sallie in them before and figured the Dawson girl must've got the loan of them, she and Sallie being the same age, size and all.

"Seems to me you fixed enough around here." Dennison was staring at her like she would disappear any minute and he'd never see her again. Me, I had a kitchen to run and better things to do than stretch the blanket. Besides, it came to me then that it was this on again-off again romance between these two that was the cause of all the disruption I was experiencing. And I found myself thinking that maybe it was time to put a stop to the whole thing.

"Actually, Mr. Haywood, it was Mr. Chisum who suggested I come out here and see you about getting some food." She was blushing a mite now and I could tell she wasn't used to having to ask for things, and to tell the truth, that suited me just fine.

"Do tell." I took a swipe at Dennison's palm with a clean cloth I was using, all the time acting as if she weren't there.

"Come now, Mr. Haywood," she said, "surely you weren't serious last night about not feeding me. Why, that's—"

"See that, lady?" I pointed to the sign I'd also mentioned last night before giving her a hard glance as I continued. "It means exactly what it says. And if you ask *Mr.* Chisum, I do believe you'll find I don't say or do nothing that ain't got a purpose to it."

"Come on, Dallas," Dennison said, "give her something to eat. She didn't mean to—"

"You're welcome to the belly-wash," I said, nodding toward the oversized coffeepot, "but you'd have to go some afore I'd figure on fixing you another meal."

She shuddered, shaking all over, only it wasn't from any morning coolness. It was rage, frustration and anything else you can conjure up that comes out of the female nature, and I'd have bet a dollar that the last person she ever did it to was her daddy. "Men!" she all but yelled, standing there like some undertaker pouring Taos Lightning into a corpse until it couldn't move. Dennison was getting a scared look about him, but I'd been through all of this before.

"That's what they call us, lady," I said to her, then, turning to Sonny, added, "First thing she's said that's right."

Now, I won't say she was outraged, but . . . well, let's just put it this way. If Turk Calder had been standing in that doorway when she stormed out, he would've been knocked over and stepped on before he knew what had hit him! Dennison was on his feet and about to go after her when I grabbed his arm, pulling him to a halt.

"Let her go," I said, watching her through the window as

she stomped off like some spoiled kid who hadn't got his way.

Then something strange happened. She was halfway to the veranda of the main house when she stopped, stock still for a moment, glanced over her shoulder at the cookshack, did an about-face as good as any soldier you've ever seen and marched right back toward us. I grabbed a flat iron just in case she got me mad enough to take her over my knee, but as it turned out I didn't need it. She stopped in front of that pile of deadwood, gave me a glare that would kill, picked up the ax and started chopping wood. I found chores for Dennison to do, but it seemed that every five minutes he was at that window, checking to see if Margaret Dawson was still chopping wood. She was. But she had the good sense to quit after half an hour. She hadn't done as much as Dennison or me or any other ranch hand would have done in that amount of time, but she'd worked off the mad she was feeling, of that I was sure.

"You think she's had enough?" Sonny asked as she put down the ax and ran a forearm across her brow. I didn't have time to answer for she charged into the room, silently did a quick survey and headed for my stove.

"Say, wait a minute, young lady, that's my—"

"I'm perfectly aware of what it is, Mr. Haywood," she said in a voice that had an edge to it. "You said you wouldn't feed me, well, fine. I'm going to feed myself." She had Kate's gumption, I'll give her that, so I stood to one side while she heated up a piece of side meat and made some eggs to go with it. I had something to say to her, but it was going to be between her and me only, so I found a chore that would take Sonny a good half-hour before he'd be finished and sent him out the door. When she threw it all onto a plate, I poured myself some coffee and lifted a foot onto the seat of the community table as she began to eat in a ravenous manner.

"Knew a fella one time," I said, sipping the steaming

liquid. "Found him a girlfriend, he did. Thought quite a bit of her too."

"Do tell," she said between bites, throwing my own barb back at me. But that made me even more determined.

"Trouble was she broke his heart when he found her in bed with his best friend. So he broke hers . . . in a manner of speaking."

"And just how did he do that?"

"Why, he shot her, of course!" I said it plain as day, as if it were the logical answer, but she almost choked on her food when I did.

"SHOT HER!" she replied when she'd cleared her throat. I handed her the cup of coffee and she swallowed half the contents but not without making a face as if it were vinegar. When she had her voice back, she gave me a serious look and said, "But why did he shoot her? What about the man she was with?"

"Oh, he couldn't shoot him. That was his best friend."

She had a puzzled look on her face now, not sure if I was serious in the telling of the story or just funning her.

"Is there some point to be made from all of this?" If there is such a thing as being cautious and formal at the same time, then Margaret Dawson was that. But then, I reckon everyone who thinks he's got some kind of so-called breeding tends to act above it all like that when he gets into a tight spot. And I do believe Miss Dawson was getting the notion that she was being maneuvered into a tight spot from which she couldn't escape.

"Yes, ma'am, there is. Point is that a man puts a good deal of trust and stock in the friends he has out here. And many a man'll tell you they're few and far between. True friends, that is."

"What about the women? I thought you cowboys all prized the women who came to this land."

"Oh we do, ma'am, we do. Fact is, a lot of 'em get fought over by the men." I set the cup down and leaned a bit closer to her, a frown forming on my forehead. "But no man likes to be played for a fool, and I'll guarantee you that ary you play Tom Lang against Sonny—or any other cowhand out here—just for the sake of being flirtatious and getting attention . . . well, you may find John Chisum sending you packing, friend of Sallie's or not." I stood back up, cocked an eyebrow at her. "Besides, that boy had something he wanted to ask you."

I tossed the cold remains of my coffee out the door and set the cup down just as she got up to leave. But when she saw me walk over to her side, she planted her git-up end back down on the seat.

"There is one other thing," I said calmly. It was what I said next that came out through grit teeth as I glared down at her. "You ever waltz in here again and start giving me orders, I'm gonna find me a hickory switch and put more calluses on that fanny of yours than you ever thought your daddy could!

"Now, you just get the hell outta here and let me do my job. You've had your fun with the hired help today."

I walked out the back door before she could leave, knowing full well that she now had the same look of awe on her face as Dennison had when she walked through the door to my kitchen that morning.

I helped Sonny out with the rest of the chores I'd given him and was back in the cookshack in half an hour. I could tell right away that something was out of place, or at least seemed out of place. You get to noticing things like that in your own haunts. The plate and fork were no longer sitting where the girl had left them, having been cleaned and placed back where they should be in my kitchen. What was sitting in their place was a piece of paper with the makings of a recipe of sorts, although I had the damnedest time making out what it was called. I reckon I never was much with a Webster's. All I knew was the handwriting, even in pencil, was the even flowing kind that women tend to have; I don't know why, but they do. And I was thinking it was likely that of Margaret Dawson.

I fiddled with it some later in the day and it wasn't half bad, no sir. Like I say, we ain't got half of the fancy stuff the city folk do, so I used my imagination and laid the spread out on the Chisums' table that night for supper.

"Say, this is pretty good, Dallas," Uncle John said, spreading some on a biscuit and taking a bite. He was acting a mite more civil than the last time we'd had a conversation. "What is it?"

I fumbled around, trying to find the paper with the recipe on it, then hesitated before reading the unpronounceable words. "You sure you want to hear?"

"Come on, Dallas," Sallie smiled, prodding me, "you know we trust you. Now, out with it."

I had the sudden urge to hightail it out of there. Don't ask me why, I just did.

"Well, one thing you folks oughtta know," I said, tossing a glance at the Dawson girl, "and that is I don't never take credit for something I can't pronounce. I made it, all right, but I'm suspicioning it come from Miss Dawson here." When I saw the red slowly creeping up her neck, I knew she was the one who'd left the recipe. Then I squinted once again at the paper. "Near as I can make out, folks, what you're eating is Horse Doovers."

"Well, I don't care what part of the horse it come off of, Dallas, it's right tasty," Chisum said.

"Let me see that," Sonny said, grabbing the piece of paper from my hand. But he could only smile at what he saw.

"Hors d'oeuvres," Margaret Dawson volunteered with a smile and a whole different pronunciation than I'd given the word.

"It's an appetizer they serve before a meal, Dallas." The Dennison boy must've been feeling his oats about then, having the upper hand like he did. But he must've seen how uncomfortable I was, for he looked over at me and smiled as he said, "It's sort of like those fish eggs without being rolled in sand, if you know what I mean."

I smiled as sheepishly as I'd ever done. "Oh yeah. Sure."

"But I must say that Mr. Haywood has done an excellent job of preparing them." This from the Dawson woman who had just taken a bite. I don't know if you've ever had the feeling that people were being more nice to you than they wanted to, but if you have . . . well, you know exactly how I was feeling then. Not that I'm much on compliments, you understand. It's just that I've been ambushed once too often not to be suspicious of things that are out of the ordinary. "Why, I'll bet Mr. Haywood rules his domain with an iron fist just to make sure it all gets done right," she said with a smile that had mischief written all over it.

"Oh yes, ma'am." Uncle John was addressing the girl but his eyes gazed right at me, a bare smile curling the corners of his mouth. "There's never been any doubt as to who runs the kitchen around the Jinglebob. Would you say, Dallas?"

Well, I didn't know what to say, so I glanced over at Margaret Dawson and made it an official truce by saying, "You can call me Dallas, ma'am."

But somehow I had the idea that I'd been unofficially told that I didn't have to worry about packing my saddlebags despite my actions. I never could figure it out. Maybe it was those horse doovers I fed them, I don't know.

Like I said, people do strange things when they get hungry.

CHAPTER EIGHT

Sometimes you can't get things to go your way for nothing. Like the time back in '46 when I was drifting south through that Brownsville area in Texas. Things hadn't been going all that well so I figured I'd try my hand south of the border. Now, everyone knew that Zack Taylor's Army of the Rio Grande had been camped down there for a year or so, so why shouldn't I be able to get safe conduct through, across to the border, even if the Mexicans and Americans weren't feeling all that good toward one another? But not me. I'm riding past a place that ain't even a place, called Palo Alto, on the far side of Taylor's infantry when all hell breaks loose up front! I mean shooting and the whole bit. Next thing I know I've got Taylor's infantry on one side of me and a bunch of wild ass Mexican lancers charging at me from the other side! If it wasn't for that handful of Rangers that lit into those lancers and the Colt and Hawken I had, why, I'd have been gone beaver!

Now, normally you might consider that an isolated incident, but after that day was over—the shooting didn't stop until near sundown—I figured I'd stay with Taylor's army overnight and see if I couldn't ride around the Mexican army the next morning. But no such luck. Oh, I swung wide of them by a couple hundred yards all right, but made the mistake of making noon camp. This time it's a place called Resaca de la Palma, a creek that ain't hardly a creek except for the springtime of the year. I'm just about ready to move on when all of the shooting starts again. There I am out in the open and here comes a couple hundred Mexican soldiers charging directly at me! The way I heard it later, they were running away from Taylor's army, but right then they looked an awful lot like they were charging right at me! Not that I'm a coward or anything, you understand, but this wasn't any of my affair to begin with, so I saddled up as fast as you ever seen and lit a shuck out of there! Never did get to Mexico.

I mention this because those two battles were the first ones fought in the Mexican War, which I never did take part in. Fact is, I hadn't thought of those two days in some time. But the way things were going, well, I couldn't help but wonder if I wasn't getting caught up in some kind of conflict that I shouldn't be in in the first place. The tension in Lincoln County was bad enough but I had that feeling in my gut that my luck now wasn't any better than it had been back in '46. First there was Turk Calder and the Dennison boy, followed by the killing of Sheriff Brady and his deputy by Billy the Kid and his friends, and my run-in with Uncle John. Yesterday it had been the Dawson girl I'd had to contend with. And even the way it turned out I still had the feeling this wasn't going to be my week.

Today wasn't any improvement on the week, not a-tall.

The Dennison boy showed up for work on time again and got through the breakfast making and eating period with a minimum of errors, all of which pleased the crew to no end. They were as cantankerous as ever toward me, but they had definitely taken a liking to Sonny. I took it as a positive sign.

It was midmorning when the Kid rode in, looking like he owned the place, and Dennison spotted him. I didn't take that for a good sign at all. Now, like I say, Chisum never turned nobody away from his place without coffee or a meal if it was on the fire, and I'd be a damn poor cook if I didn't at least have coffee ready day or night. So I poured some black water for the Kid and handed him the cup, hoping the other half of Lincoln that was likely looking for him wouldn't show up just then.

"Thanks, cookie." He was slow getting off his horse, winced a mite once he placed the game leg on the ground, but soon had that affable smile on his face when he sipped my coffee. I reckon that's one thing about the Kid; those that understand him can't help but like him, while those that don't care one way or another purely hate his guts. Me, I'd tolerate him as long as it wasn't me he was shooting at. Dennison, on the other hand, treated him like a long-lost friend.

"I thought I had you butchering some meat out back," I said in a stern voice when the boy suddenly appeared at my side, saying his howdy-do's to the Kid.

"Almost done," he said, but it was the Kid he was eyeing as he said it. "Say, you wouldn't mind if, uh . . . well, you know what I—"

I knew what he meant.

"If you ain't got nothing to do, Kid, don't do it around here. There's work to be done." I'd been telling Dennison this boy-man wasn't one to tangle with and that might be so, but he was in my domain now and I don't care who you are when I've got work to be done.

"Well, then, you don't mind if I do it around back, do you, Dallas?" The smile was mischievous, the kind that said he was determined to have his way. "Besides, if you refill this cup, I'll be able to account to my stomach for both breakfast and lunch. And I won't bother your assistant."

Grudgingly, I refilled the cup and said nothing more, although I did keep an eye out the back window to see that Dennison was doing his job. Oddly enough, the boy was able to do two things at one time and actually did finish up his butchering a short time later, something I would have strongly doubted a few days back. The boy was pumping Billy for everything he could get on how to be a fast draw, purely fascinated by the Kid's stories.

"Do you really think you could teach me, Billy?" I heard him ask in awe as the two moved out front again.

"Sure, nothing to it."

By the time I got to the entrance, the Kid was showing off the kind of stuff that has absolutely nothing to do with the shooting of a pistol. Drawing the pistol and twirling it, the border shift, the road agent's spin, all of that stuff Cody had Hickok doing in his first Wild West show back in '73.

It was when I walked through the door that I knew it was going to be another one of those days.

"Fancy stuff, Kid, but can you shoot?" It wasn't a question as much as a challenge, and it came from Tom Lang, who'd just ridden in. The Kid had the pistol back in his holster and spun around right fast for having a hitch in his git along. But then, I would've too if Lang had ridden up behind me like he just did the Kid.

"I don't think I know you," Billy said, squinting in the sunlight. "Why don't you get down off your horse." He was smiling now and that bothered Lang as he slowly dismounted.

There was trouble brewing, of that I was sure, and if these two hardheads went up against each other you could bet hell would take a holiday. They couldn't have been more than ten or twelve feet apart and you could see it in their eyes that they were ready to go at one another. Me, I was standing between them and off to the side some. And you'd better believe that pulling my bowie knife got the attention of both of them.

"Now, this here, Sonny, is what you call a couple of Daniel Boones." The boy was standing off to my side somewhere, although I couldn't see him at the moment. "Yup. They'll fight at the drop of the hat just so's they can prove they're tougher than nails. What these two pilgrims don't know is that the survivor of this fandango"—here I glanced back and forth at each with a smile that Jim Bridger once described as devilish mean—"well, I'm gonna cut his heart out and feed it to him while he dies."

"Can't say as I'd blame you, Dallas." This comment came from Uncle John as he approached us. "Now, just what is going on here?" When Lang, the Kid and Sonny all started talking at once, Uncle John held up a hand, a stern look about him. "I believe I was asking Dallas that question."

"Lang decided he needed to show us how tough he is again," I said. "And this youngster was ready to oblige him, it seems." It didn't make either of the two any too happy.

"That's a goddamn—"

"Lang," Chisum said, cutting him off, "it seems to me I hired you to work with my crew, not act like some south of the border *pistolero*. Now what is it you came in for?"

"We didn't have enough branding irons, so I come in for a couple more." His brow was furrowed to say the least, and if he hadn't been afraid of losing his job, I do believe the words would have come out through grit teeth. Instead, they were just hard and flat, those of a man talking to his superior.

"Then get 'em and get back out to the roundup."

"Yes, sir." Lang was a tough nut, all right, but he knew what his boundaries were when it came to going up against the boss. He gave the Kid a hard glare and walked off.

When Lang was gone, Chisum turned to the Kid, slowly sizing him up. "Mr. Bonney, isn't it?"

The Kid just gave him that laconic smile of his and shrugged. "Some say."

"Well, now, Mr. Bonney, I hope you didn't come out here to start any trouble." Uncle John cocked his head at Billy as though to convey that he didn't believe him to be all that innocent in what was nearly a shoot-out. "I won't allow that on the Jinglebob."

"Actually, Mr. Chisum, I was figuring on stopping some trouble more than starting it."

"That so." The Kid had all three of us interested in how

he was going to do that. That I recollect, one-man armies never do last too awful long. Something about lack of support.

"Sure is. I heard in Lincoln you had a fella do some writing for you so's to straighten this mess out with the Murphy-Dolan crowd."

"Yes," John said, "that's true. So far."

"Well, the mails are awful slow, Mr. Chisum, and there ain't no telling how long those letters will take to get back East."

"Get to the point, son."

"Point is I figure I could take care of some of your problems a whole lot quicker, if you had a mind to put me on the payroll." Dennison's eyes lit up at the thought of having Billy the Kid working side by side with him at the same outfit. Trouble was I doubted that the Kid had ever peeled that many spuds in his life—or had any intention to. He sure wasn't hiring on for the spring roundup, and John Chisum·knew that as well as I did.

"Well, son, I'll tell you, what you do is your own affair," the tall rancher drawled. A serious look came to his face as he eyed Billy. "But the truth is I never have taken to hired guns to handle my problems. This is a working ranch and the work involves a bit more sweat than what you'd mussed up on the palm of your hand, son. I know John Tunstall thought a lot of you and I can understand how you feel about his death, but no thanks, Mr. Bonney, I'm not hiring gunmen to do my dirty work." Then, with a nod of the head, he said, "Now, if you'll excuse me, I have a ranch to run." He didn't wait for a reply, simply turned to head back to the main house before stopping in his tracks. He did a half right, the way a man will when he's half on his way and has just remembered something forgotten. "Oh, and Mr. Bonney?"

"Sir?"

"You're welcome to the coffee or food that's available

when we serve it. But if you want to chew the fat, maybe you ought to make your visits around supper time, toward the end of the day."

"Sir?" This time the voice sounded as confused as the face looked.

"What he means is plant your git up end on that saddle and point your horse in a direction that's headed away from the Jinglebob," I said in a stern manner.

"I'd say that's as good an interpretation as I've ever heard, Dallas. Yes, I do." Then he was on his way back to the main house.

The Kid slowly mounted his horse and gave one last glance at the back of Chisum as he disappeared into the house.

"Strange fella."

"Ain't we all," I said.

"See you later, Sonny," the Kid said with a smile. "Remember what I told you."

"Billy?" The Kid was reining his horse to go when Dennison spoke up, having to ask just one more question.

"Yeah."

"Why'd you tell Lang to get off his horse?" It was one of those simple questions a pilgrim will ask in a simple way. And that was Dennison, all right.

"Oh, that." The Kid smiled in that way he had. "It's sort of the law of the land, Sonny. You gotta give 'em a fair chance in a shoot-out. Let's just say I didn't want anyone saying I'd taken advantage of him when I killed him. *Hasta la vista.*"

He took his time riding out but if I hadn't dragged Dennison back into the cookshack I do believe he'd have been there at sundown still watching the dust on the horizon.

"Ain't he something?" the boy asked as we set back to work. He had that same look of awe that he got when the Dawson girl was around.

"And just how do you figure that?" It never ceased to

amaze me how dumb some of these pilgrims could get. In the case of Sonny, I was getting pure flustered my own self. Hell, one minute the boy was acting like he had some savvy about this land and the next he was acting like he'd just got off the stage, bowler hat and all.

"Why, he offered Mr. Chisum a hand in this war you say is brewing, and stood up to Tom Lang too." The way he said it he held nothing but admiration for Billy the Kid, hero at large. "And he would have taken Lang fair and square, you heard him!"

"Seems to me you've got an awful short memory, son." I'd about had it with hero worship for the day, not to mention Daniel Boone would-be gunfighters.

"Well, he said it was—"

"The law of the land," I interrupted. "Sure, I know, I know. And I won't say that he's totally wrong in what he says about that fair shake stuff, but that's where your memory falls short, if you ask me."

"How?" I seemed to truly have the boy confused.

"The Kid may have given Lang a fair shake today," I said, looking him square in the eye. "But ain't you forgetting that it was only a couple of days ago that he killed the sheriff and his deputy? And ambushing a man ain't anything close to fair or the law of the land."

"Oh." It was all the boy could say.

Fact is, I didn't hear anything else about Billy the Kid all that day.

CHAPTER NINE

There is no end of the week for cooks. There are just seven days in the week that you get up and do the same thing, and unless you're a stickler for how much work you do, you simply mark off the days on the calendar and keep on working. Most days, that is. The day after Billy the Kid and Tom Lang nearly killed one another was sort of a half workday for me, and you can bet it wasn't Woodrow Dennison who was doing the work for me!

When Sonny showed up there was something strange about him. It wasn't that he was lackadaisical about what he did as much as it was something that was weighing on his mind.

"Come on, Sonny, you ain't still thinking about the Kid and what happened yesterday, are you?" He knew what I'd said, but seemed to be in another land, another place and time. He shrugged.

"I guess I am." At least he admitted it.

"Well, get it outta your mind, youngster," I said in a half growl, knowing I'd have his attention then, " 'cause in 'bout an hour Lang and his crew are gonna be in here, and as much as they seem to like you, I can guarantee they're gonna unlike you ary their bellies ain't satisfied. Besides, the Kid's likely out of the country by now."

"I doubt it," he said in a lower than normal voice, as he busied himself in the shack.

"What was that?"

"Oh, nothing."

It seemed odd that the boy would say such a thing, for

the obvious line of thought was that Billy Bonney was now on the wanted list for killing the sheriff and his deputy and, if he had any brains at all, would head south of the border until things cooled off. To tell the truth, I was a mite surprised when he'd showed up at the Jinglebob the day before. On the other hand, not much of what you'd normally call obvious was happening around here of late. And if you ask me, there wasn't anybody I'd met in the past week that was using too much horse sense, and I'd include myself in that group too! Still, what the boy said stuck in my craw that morning.

"Uncle John says he'd like you to make some more of those *hors d'oeuvres* for supper tonight." Lang and his crew had already left and Dennison was out back doing more of the heavy work while I tried to enjoy what was comparative silence in my own kitchen. Maybe that's why her voice startled me.

"Don't do that," I said, just a bit annoyed.

"What? Why?"

"Walking up behind a man is *what*," I said, getting a mite tired of having to cater to explaining life in the West to pilgrims, no matter how pretty they were. " 'Cause you'll wind up getting yourself killed is the *why*."

"But I only—"

"You walk up behind a man who makes his living with a gun and you may never live to tell your grandchildren about it. Some of those critters'd rather shoot first and ask questions later." The scene between Lang and the Kid yesterday immediately came to mind as I spoke. "And the way things are going around here lately, I wouldn't say as I'd blame 'em," I added, not sure she was aware of the feud taking place. "By the way, you see Sonny out back on the way over?"

"Yes," she said, although I'd swear that smile of hers was about as fragile as the girl herself. "He said to tell you he'd be through in about half an hour."

"Sounds 'bout his speed," I commented, shaking my head. "Boy's had an addled brain all morning." I went back to work, but the girl simply stood in the doorway. When she didn't leave, I glanced over my shoulder at her. "You keep standing there like that and I'm gonna put you to work."

She gave me that weak smile again. "Work wasn't exactly what I had in mind."

"Oh?" She had my interest now. Looking at her, I felt an urge I hadn't felt since . . . well, since.

"Dallas," she said in a tone that had seduction in it, "I don't suppose you'd care to swap recipes with an Eastern cook like me?"

Bingo! Swapping recipes between cooks is better than being seduced! Well, almost. I poured her some coffee and invited her to sit down to palaver. We must've sat there for a good half-hour talking recipes, except it was me doing all the talking. I was telling her how we make sonofabitch stew, and fricassee rattlesnake and . . . well, you know, all of the dishes we consider to be delicacies out here. I was getting ready to refill my coffee cup when I pulled out the watch I carried. Normally you can tell how much time has gone by, but when you get to palavering it sort of gets away from you.

"I'd better check on Dennison," I said, placing the watch back in its fob. "Still got work to do here."

When I went out back it was evident that the boy had done his work and cleaned up, but he was nowhere in sight. I called his name out a couple of times, even used his real name once, figuring that would flush him out if nothing else would, but I got no answer. Then it struck me. Something the Kid had said to Dennison yesterday about not forgetting and the boy's behavior this morning didn't seem right. Now, I'm no Edgar Allan Poe detective or even a Pinkerton agent, but putting puzzles together of late seemed to be my second occupation.

"Where is he?" I said, storming back into the kitchen the

same way Margaret Dawson had left the other day. The difference was that she had the good sense to take note of the mad on my face when I stopped right in front of her. That smile of hers had been weak because it was as false as a saloon front in a mining camp. But it had been replaced now with a look of fear.

"Please don't be mad." She was on the verge of crying, or at least had the look, and that's something I never could tell for sure on a woman. But whether it was real or not, Miss Margaret Dawson was about to find out that working your way out of a tight spot takes more than good looks.

"Mad! Me, MAD!" I do believe she figured I was about to foam at the mouth when I said that. "I got a kitchen to run and you sit here stretching the blanket with me just so's the pilgrim can sneak away without me knowing 'bout it, and you got the gall to tell me not to be mad!!" I threw the old beaver hat I wore down on the table hard enough to give it some movement. "Missy, I was calmer the last time I fought a griz!" From the look about her she must've gone from fear to shock. "Now, where the hell is he!"

"He said it was something he had to do," she mumbled between sobs. Then, in a forlorn look that was filled with pure amazement, she added, "He said you'd understand." Crying is something else I've never been able to figure out about women, and that was what she was doing now. Hell, you'd have thought she was watering the rose garden, as much water as flowed down her cheeks.

"I still need to know where he went." I wasn't yelling this time, but when she looked up I reckon she knew there wasn't a whole hell of a lot of sorry I was feeling for her.

"Some place called Blazer's Mill," she replied as I handed her my kerchief. The banks of the river were receding and the water flow turned to a trickle. With red eyes, she said, "He said he was going there with that Billy boy, whatever his name is."

"Billy the Kid?" I frowned as things began to make sense

in an odd sort of way. Dennison knew where the Kid was going to be today, likely figuring on being there himself, which he probably was right now.

"Yes, that's him, that's the one."

"Horse apples!" I undid the apron I had on and checked the Greener I grabbed up from the corner. It was taking up that shotgun that made her realize the situation was more serious than she might have envisioned.

"You don't think there's going to be any trouble, do you?"

"You can bet your git up end and everything else attached to it on that, young lady."

"Then I'll go with you!" All of a sudden she had a lot of heart, just like some mustangs I've ridden. The difference was that the Dawson girl's gumption came from guilt. "I feel so responsible for what's happened."

She was making her way to the door, but as soon as I sloshed on my hat I had a firm grip on her shoulder and all her feet were doing was digging up the ground as they moved.

"Oh no, you don't," I said, spinning her around. "You ain't getting out of this that easy. No walking away from it this time, missy." She gave me one of those how-dare-you looks, but I really didn't care because the feeling was mutual. I took a hold of her elbow and guided her over to the stove. "You seemed to do fair to middling the other day on short notice, feeding yourself. Now, let's see what you can do for a good-sized crew."

"You're insane!"

"That's right, lady. One of the requirements of the job." I headed for the doorway, Margaret Dawson standing there with as perplexed a look as you'd ever see.

"But what am I going to cook?" she asked hopelessly.

"Meat's out back. Use your imagination." I squinted, offered her a brief smile. "You seem right good at that."

"But—"

"Tell you what, missy, why don't you make up some of them fancy horse doovers for the boys? That oughtta take the edge off their appetites."

I wasn't but five steps out the door when I heard her yell, "But what do I feed them?!!" When I turned around there she was, as frustrated as I'd intended her to be.

"Well, now, ma'am, less'n you've got some ideas, I'd say that six-shooter coffee in there is about your only hope." Her face turned as red as a beet and I knew if she'd had a cleaver in her hand she'd likely have tried doing me in, especially when I smiled at her. You know what I mean. It's the kind of smile you give a body when you know you've had the last word and he—or she in this case—knows you know it. "But don't worry, you're pretty. The boys won't be too hard on you."

Walking toward the corral I knew for a fact that the next time I saw Miss Dawson at least her ears wouldn't be virginal anymore.

CHAPTER TEN

Like I said, this just wasn't my week. Dennison was the first decent help I'd had around that kitchen for some time and all he'd turned out to be was hell with the hide off, more trouble than he was worth. Teaming up with *anything* that had to do with Billy the Kid was turning out to be pure death of late, and I don't mind telling you that I didn't like it, not one bit. By God, if someone was going to shoot Sonny, it was going to be me!

Riding out of there I wasn't sure if I was going to take on the Kid for convincing Dennison to meet him someplace or not. Maybe I'd just beat him to a pulp, which wouldn't be hard considering that he was as sawed off as me and three times as skinny. I reckon what really stuck in my craw was what Sonny'd let the Dawson girl in for. Getting her to stall me while he took off and telling her that I'd understand to boot really took the cake. And if I didn't make it back before the evening meal was prepared, I knew for sure that she was going to have second thoughts about Dennison, romance or no romance. Fact is, it was almost enough to make me feel sorry for her, but almost don't count out here except in horseshoes and near miss target practice.

I never was much for wearing spurs; always figured that if you wanted to butcher a horse you oughtta wait till it's dead and use a good cleaver. But that mustang I was riding gave a good hard ride with the nudging of my heels as I headed for Blazer's Mill.

It wasn't that I was in such an all-fired hurry to get back to the preparation of the evening meal as it was one single, solitary thought that stuck in the back of my mind. I was remembering what the Kid had said that day in Kate's store about how he and Fred Waite set up the ambush that finally killed Sheriff Brady and Hindman, neither of which I had any love for. But the way he said it I knew he'd enjoyed it, and that's what was bothering me now. What if he'd invited this pilgrim, Dennison, to another ambush he was setting up? What if Sonny was figuring he had to participate in something like that to show the crew of the Jinglebob that he was a real man? It wouldn't be the first time some misguided youth had tried entering manhood that way. Trouble was that most of them wound up being the subject of some circuit-riding sky pilot who said a few kind words before they got buried.

Blazer's Mill is somewhat east by south of Lincoln, depending on how you ride, but from the Chisum spread I had a ways to go. It is comprised of some six or eight buildings and borders the Mescalero Reservation at the foot of the Sacramento Mountains. When I rode in I knew there was trouble. I was too far away to spot Sonny, but offhand it looked to be about a dozen men or so standing out there in the open. Riding in like that I had a feeling I knew how Custer must've felt at the Little Big Horn.

"Well, now, boys, having parties at midday are you?" I asked, trying to be as sociable and easygoing as possible. I'd walked my horse in the last hundred yards and was now glad I had. From the serious looks on the faces of the men there, I'd likely have been shot without question as an intruder if I'd ridden in hell-for-leather. Without waiting for an answer I found Dennison in the crowd, gave him a hard glance, then an even harder one when I saw the Colt .44-40 and shell belt he was wearing. They were mine! "You and me gotta talk, son," was all I said to him.

"Buckshot Roberts showed up just after we did, Mr. Haywood," a young, curly-haired man named Dick Brewer said. I'd known Brewer as a farmer until John Tunstall had gotten killed. Since then he'd become the leader of a group seeking revenge for the killing of Tunstall who called themselves the "Regulators." Billy the Kid was and wasn't a member of this force, which seemed logical in an odd sort of way since he pretty much did what he wanted these days. "Frank Coe knows him, so I sent him in to talk to him, see can we take him in without any shooting."

"I see," I said, dismounting and leading my horse out of harm's way. The last thing I needed—next to a dead cook's helper—was a dead horse.

Andrew L. "Buckshot" Roberts was nothing but trouble. He might have been about my age and size and was feisty as all get out, but he was trouble just the same. Depending on whose story you believed, Roberts was an ex-soldier, Indian fighter, and former Texas Ranger—or none of them. He'd gotten the nickname by being peppered with a shotgun that had given him a game shoulder. And for my money, the fellow on the firing end of that shotgun was likely an ex-soldier, Indian fighter or Texas Ranger—if you get the drift of what I mean. Some people have a strange way of turning the circumstances of their life around. Word had it that there was a two-hundred-dollar bounty being put out on the killers of Brady and Hindman by the Lincoln County commissioners. The wording "dead or alive" on that order may well have given Roberts the idea that he could pick up some easy money by tracking down the Kid, Fred Waite and a few of Brewer's crowd. What Roberts may have forgotten was that there was a John Doe warrant still out for the killers of John Tunstall, and it was pretty well suspicioned that he was one of the crowd who had killed the Lincoln rancher.

Leading my horse off, I spotted Coe and Roberts on the west side of the main house Dr. Joseph Blazer worked out of. I'd also gotten close enough to hear what they were saying. .

"Give me your rifle," Frank Coe was telling Roberts,

"and we'll walk around to the crowd. I'll stand by you whatever happens." Coe was supposed to have known Roberts from somewhere so Brewer had made a good choice in finding someone to talk peaceable to him. But Roberts wasn't having any of it.

"Surrender?" he replied. "Never, while I'm alive. Kid Antrim is with you and he'd kill me on sight. Don't I know what happened to Morton and Baker?"

Kid Antrim was another summer name Billy the Kid had, along with his Billy Bonney alias. And Roberts was probably right, the Kid likely would kill him on sight, as strongly as he felt about the death of John Tunstall. As for Morton and Baker, well, they were two of the plug uglies who were supposed to have been in the mob that killed Tunstall, along with Roberts and the rest of the Jesse Evans gang. They'd conveniently showed up dead about a month ago and in the possession of Dick Brewer. The coroner pretty much ruled that they had died of an extreme case of lead poisoning, although they never could pin the murders on Brewer or his bunch. No, I couldn't rightly blame Buckshot Roberts for saying what he did, no, sir.

Still, Frank Coe stood there for a while, trying to convince Roberts that he ought to lay down his arms and come in peacefully. After all, a dozen to one odds in any kind of fight never are too smart. But Roberts wasn't moving, not one inch.

I was more taken by the conversation between Roberts and Coe than what was going on with Brewer's crowd, so it was a surprise when I saw Charlie Bowdre, George Coe— Frank's cousin—and a third man approach the two men as they talked. For one instant I thought I saw the look of a man being betrayed flash in Roberts' eyes, but by then I reckon even he knew it was too late.

"Roberts, throw up your hands," Bowdre called out, but like I say, Roberts wasn't having any.

"No!" was his defiant reply.

That game shoulder kept Roberts from firing his rifle like most of us would, but he knew how to hit his mark firing from the waist. He was bringing his rifle to bear when Bowdre pulled his six-gun and gut shot him. Now, hoss, you don't take a gut shot any too well, but Roberts had more sand than these lads had figured on. He made his way back to the doorway of Blazer's house while the rest of these yahoos found something to hide behind. Once inside he had somehow dragged what looked like a mattress up to the front door, enabling him to stand there and fire from the prone position. It was then I realized that even spectators were fair game in this shoot-out and headed for the cover of a wagon standing near the side of the main house. I had no intention of rushing Roberts or even tangling with him for that matter. I just said a silent prayer that Brewer's crowd didn't mistake me for Roberts!

You'd have thought they were fighting the Battle of Gettysburg all over again, as much lead as was flying through the air! Most of the gunfire came from Winchester rifles and Colt pistols, but when I heard a couple of louder, more forceful shots, I knew Roberts had taken hold of Dr. Blazer's Springfield rifle, a .45-60 that he stocked a goodly amount of ammunition for. If these boys were figuring on moving in on Roberts after he ran out of ammunition, they had another think coming.

Most of the Brewer crowd had taken cover behind a cut bank to the front of the house, a couple of them wounded on the way. Believe me, you can tell when a man trips or takes a dive on purpose from when he's thrown down by a bullet. It simply isn't a natural movement.

About the time it seemed like everyone had emptied their guns, I saw three men make a rush in two different directions. One of them was Dick Brewer himself, successfully taking up a position about forty-five degrees to the right of the others behind some large logs near the sawmill. The other two were Billy the Kid and Sonny, heading straight for me! The Kid's leg wasn't all that well healed from the wound he'd taken in the Brady killing, but something told me that the flinch he made wasn't from anything being wrong with his leg. Surprisingly, they both made it to the wagon relatively unharmed. Dennison hadn't been touched at all, but the Kid was bleeding from what appeared to be nothing more than a graze on the arm.

"Seems anymore I meet you, you're bleeding from a new wound," I said, yanking my kerchief out and tying it around his arm, shirt sleeve and all. But it didn't seem to phase him at all.

"Thought you could use some company," he said with that same reckless smile I'd seen before.

"What's Brewer trying to do, get hisself killed?" I asked in a tone of voice that let him know I wasn't any too thrilled about this whole experience.

"Trying to get a better shot at Roberts." The smile was gone now as he reloaded. "You know, that fella's a damn good shot. I don't know if he did it on purpose or not, but one of his loads took off Charlie Bowdre's gun belt, and another took off George Coe's trigger finger at the first joint."

"Face it, Kid, you've met your match. Another show-off in the country besides you. But don't worry," I added, tapping the kerchief, watching him silently flinch, "I think he was serious about killing you."

"Look!" It was the first thing Dennison had said since I'd been here, but his fascination was directed at Brewer, who was slowly raising his head to take aim at Roberts. Hell, maybe he had found a better shooting position, or at least a clearer shot at the man who was their nemesis. Trouble was Brewer never made it. It was maybe a hundred and fifty feet from the house to where he was situated behind those logs, but my eyes aren't that bad yet. If a pilgrim like Dennison could spot him, I knew good and well that Buckshot Roberts could too, dying or not.

And he did.

That Springfield went off with a boom and Dick Brewer's head and hat went flying back, but not before I saw what looked to be a gigantic black spot just above the center of his eyes.

"You're right, Kid, he's a damn good shot."

That one shot did it, stopped the whole shooting war just like that. It was almost as if everything had been decided with that one boom of Roberts' Springfield. And in a way it had. There was general confusion among the Regulators, a lot of men looking at one another, not knowing what to do now that their leader was gone. I don't think the Kid could believe it either but he kept his guard up. As for Dennison . . . well, he just stared at the place Brewer's head once was and turned a sickly shade of green around the gills.

"I never seen a man get killed before." The excitement his face had earlier displayed about this adventure was now replaced with a look filled with remorse and regret. All I had to do was look at his eyes and I could see him envisioning the bloody mass that lay behind those logs, knew it wouldn't be long before he got sick to his stomach. When he did, I turned to the Kid, feeling a mite of hatred my own self.

"Some gunfighter," I said to him. If I sounded harsh, it's because I felt that way. "Look at him, upchucking everything. Is that what you brought him up here for? Teach him how to show off like you do?"

Those words hurt him, likely because he knew they were true for the most part. It wasn't that I disliked the Kid, for I didn't. It was just that you had to get used to him, sort of like that horrible cure-all your mama gave you when you were a youngster. You had to take it in doses, and I'd about had my fill of Kid Antrim, Billy Bonney or anything else you wanted to call him—at least for now.

"I brought him up here to teach him how to use a gun," he said. "That's all, cookie. Believe me, I didn't know

Brewer and his men were gonna be here." He paused a moment, gave a quick glance to where the men he'd just spoken of were and saw that they were saddling up, wounded and all. "What the—" he started to say, then took off, running hell-for-leather for his own horse. He made it without a shot being fired and rode off with the others, leaving Dick Brewer's body where it had been slain.

Watching them ride off, I had the feeling that it was Roberts who'd put the fear of God in them more than the other way around. That reminded me that there was still a wounded, desperate man I had to deal with before I got out of here unharmed and he likely wasn't feeling too neighborly. My shotgun was still loaded, unfired, so I set it down, silently cautioning Dennison to stay where he was at as I worked my way around to the front door. By the time I got there I had my bowie in hand, my back flattened against the wall peppered with numerous bullet holes.

"Roberts, this is Dallas Haywood. I ain't packing iron and I ain't got nothing against you, understand? So whatever artillery you're holding, I'd appreciate it ary you'd set it down. Let me in and I might be able to help you. Deal?" If he wanted to kill me, he could've shot right through the wall with that Springfield and done me in; let's just say I was counting on him being desperate enough to want to live.

He was. I heard a weak reply and moved inside the door quickly, but I needn't have worried. The man was slumped against the back of it looking like death warmed over. He saw the bowie, began to slowly shake his head back and forth, apparently figuring I was going to finish what Brewer and his men had started. It was then Sonny showed up in the doorway, a curious look crossing his face as he saw the bowie too.

"Oh no you don't," I said to him before he took a step toward me. "Come in here and you'll lose your breakfast all over again. You just amble on out there and get us our horses and get ready to ride." When he threw me a challenging look I gave it right back to him. "The day ain't over yet." That gave him something to think about as he walked off.

"You want to do anything for him, you'd best get the post physician over to Fort Stanton," I said when Doc Blazer came forward. He agreed the wound was a serious one, likely even fatal, but sent word for a doctor. Maybe that gave Roberts some brief moment of hope in hearing that, but I think both Blazer and me knew that the only thing that was going to keep the pain down in the man before us was a good, heavy dose of Taos Lightning.

If silence was golden, Dennison and me should have been rich beyond our wildest dreams by the time we got back to the Jinglebob, for all we did was ride like the wind, the only thing exchanged being a couple of hard glares at one another. By the time we pulled up in front of the cookshack I knew good and well this tall youngster I'd ridden with had a genuine need to try taking a piece of my hide, whether he thought he could or not.

"Tend to these horses and get back to me soon as you can," I said, tossing him my reins. But riding with the Kid and Brewer must've given him some confidence 'cause he tossed them right back at me.

"Just who do you think—" It wasn't confidence coming out now but loud mouth, the same as Turk Calder.

"Lemme tell you something, Sonny," I said, slapping the reins in one of his hands while I jabbed a stubby finger into his chest. "I'm 'bout fed up with being sassed by you youngsters today. Now, you got a beef with me, you just come at me." I glared at him like I'd done to no one in a long time. "But get the goddamn horses took care of first. They worked harder than you have today."

I walked off before he had a chance to reply, hoping I could salvage what hadn't been done to the evening meal.

But to my surprise, the crew was happy as could be at the community table. It didn't look like they'd been served a hell of a lot of food, but they sure looked happy about it, whatever it was.

"What's going on?" I pushed back my hat and cocked a suspicious eye at the lot of them. Then I saw Margaret Dawson bring out a pot of coffee and knew instinctively that every one of those punchers was going to ask for a refill just so he could smile up into her face. "Never mind," I muttered, and made my way to the back, setting the Greener back in its resting place.

After a bit of snooping around, I could only surmise that Lang's crew had been satisfied with eating half of the normal amount of food I usually prepared for them, for only that much of the butchered beef had been used. Looking at a pretty girl serving it must've made up for whatever else their stomachs missed.

"You should be proud of me, Dallas," she said with a pleasing smile, setting the coffeepot down. I didn't know how she did it, but she'd fed these yahoos and gotten away with it and that was enough for me.

"I am," I growled.

"Then why aren't you smiling?"

"Because of me." Dennison said it from the entrance of the cookshack, almost as if he wanted the whole outfit to know about it. Everyone heard it as all eyes went from Sonny to me, all silently waiting for a reaction. It was a shame the boy hadn't learned any more than how to run his mouth that day.

"That's right, because of you." I was still growling, still feeling mean as hell. I get that way when I've gone a full day and don't think I've accomplished one hell of a lot. So far all I'd done was pull Dennison's bacon out of the fire in a roundabout way of speaking. Truth to tell, about then I was ready to *fry* it!

"Buckshot Roberts got gut shot this morning out at Blazer's Mill," I said to the boys as I made my way past them to Dennison. That set them to gabbing in low voices like a bunch of old hens, but they stopped when I added, "Dick Brewer bought the farm, too." There were some incredulous looks among them, for although Brewer was a farmer and cattlemen generally don't like farmers, he was also looking to right a wrong that had been done, namely the murder of John Tunstall.

"What you did this morning was dumb, kid." I'd positioned myself in front of him now, the entrance to his back as I shoved the flat of my hand into his chest. It pushed him back, his head hitting the cross bar of the entrance doorway, a look that was somewhere between pain and anger coming to his face. "You could have gotten killed."

"Oh, my God." The panicky voice was Margaret Dawson's to my rear and I only had to hear it to know what she regretted doing this morning. I'd deal with her later, but Dennison needed tending to right now.

He must've thought I was going to hit him again for he backed out of the cookshack, which was just what I'd wanted him to do. You don't seriously think I was going to allow any fighting in my own establishment, do you?

"But you disappointed me, kid. You stole my gun and lied to me." He was turning red-faced now, whether it was because I'd just spoken the truth or because I dared to say it in front of the outfit I don't know. I glanced over my shoulder at the crew I knew was listening to every word. "He ain't one helluva gunfighter, either."

It was as effective as waving a red flag at an already mad bull. The fire in his eyes was pure hatred now as he raised his right hand and took a wide roundhouse punch at me. Except he didn't. I caught hold of his forearm as it came down at me and drove my own into his brisket, a sure way to give a body that sick around the gills feeling. He must've been expecting it for he didn't fall that far forward. But it gave me enough time to let go of his right arm and bring a short jab to his jaw as I let loose my own roundhouse punch. It sent him sprawling, although it didn't knock him out. As many times as he'd been hit the last week, maybe his jaw was getting used to it. But the fire in him hadn't died, not yet.

"Don't talk to me about lying," he said to me from the ground, speaking as mad as he looked. "You told Roberts you weren't packing iron, but I saw you with that knife!"

Now, friend, you just don't do that out here without expecting some kind of results and before Dennison could move I had that bowie knife stuck in a piece of wood he'd landed by some six inches from his head. And you can bet it was me doing the hard talking now!

"*That*, youngster, is forged out of *steel!*" I said, glaring down at him. I was right and he knew I was, but he was too damned hardheaded to admit it.

"I still say—"

"Never call a man a liar just because he knows more'n you do. It's the biggest cause of lead poisoning that I know of out here," I said. I heard one of the crew chuckle some, but I hadn't said it to be funning anyone. "You call me a liar again, Dennison, and I'm gonna take your ears off just like Jack Slade done to Jules Reni."

No one laughed at that, likely because I wasn't joshing about a feud that had become a bit of a legend out here and the results of it. Slade had done to Reni just what I said he had, using one ear for a watch fob and hanging the other above the door to the relay station he ran as a warning to other intruders who might take a notion to pushing him too far.

I only had one moment of fear then and it was when the boy, most likely realizing he had been humiliated in front of most of the Chisum ranch crew, made one last stab at having his way. His hand went for that Colt of mine that he wore and I thought sure I was gone beaver!

"You have to take the thong off the hammer first, Sonny,"

Tom Lang said as the boy unsuccessfully pulled again and again at the holstered pistol. I hadn't seen him around at all, but there he was, slipping the thong off his own Peace-maker. "Of course, if you do that and you pull that gun . . . well, I can guarantee you you'll never see the sun come up tomorrow. At least not in this world."

The boy knew he meant it. Hell, *everybody* knew he meant it! Sometimes it ain't the way a man looks at you but the tone of his voice that lets you know he means business, and with Tom Lang right then that was how it was.

"All right, boys, that's it," he said after it became appar-ent that Dennison was taking Lang's advice. "If you're through eating, move on." Then, to Sonny, "I suspicion our cook's helper's got hisself some clean-up work to do."

I sheathed the bowie and took my gun belt from Denni-son as the crowd dispersed, leaving just Lang, me and the boy.

"Well, what do you know, it is yours," Lang said, recog-nizing, just as I had that morning, the small chunk of wood missing from the lower right hand grip of the gun. I gave him a warning glance, having had enough fighting for one day, and he turned his attention to Dennison. "You know, son, sometimes it's better to pull your freight than pull your gun."

"More Western wisdom?"

"Right outta Shakespeare as I hear it." And it was for a fact; we just interpret things a bit differently than those Eastern pilgrims do. When the boy finally realized it just wasn't his day and left, the foreman said he had other duties to attend to and began walking away.

"Tom." He stopped after a half dozen steps, likely more surprised than anything for I'd seldom called him by his first name.

"Yeah."

"Thanks. I'm much obliged. If there's ever—"

"As a matter of fact, there is, Dallas. Next time you feed

the crew don't hold back on 'em. You see I can hear their stomachs just a-growling from way out here." He said it in his normal voice, but I had the feeling there was just a mite of humor in it . . . maybe even the offering of a peace pipe, if you know what I mean.

"Bank on it."

Having that conversation reminded me that I hadn't had anything to eat since breakfast and my own stomach started to growl. It seemed like it had been a day for growling and such.

CHAPTER ELEVEN

The next couple of days weren't what you'd call memorable for the feelings of a cook and his helper toward one another, but Tom Lang's crew got fed, and on time. The Dennison boy acted more like he'd lost his voice as we worked, but he did his job, grudgingly at first, but he did it. I got the impression he was losing his yearning for being a real-life cowhand, maybe even contemplating going back East. Me, I was beginning to think that might be where he belonged all along.

His popularity with the crew had dropped some too and that likely hurt him the most. After all, for all his good intentions all he'd been doing since he got here was stepping in it, and you don't have to be but a newborn of anything to amble around the barnyard doing that. That's the trouble with humans, the damn fools get their feelings hurt too easy. And after what had happened . . . well, I reckon everyone on the Chisum spread knew that Dennison was a damn fool, especially Dennison.

"Don't you think you were a bit too hard on him?" the Dawson girl asked the day after it was all over. Sonny was out back again, tending to chores I'd given him.

"Missy," I said, stopping what I was doing and giving her one hellacious hard look, "ary I'd wanted to be *hard* on him, I'd have done it in front of the Kid and them so-called Regulators, but they taken off quicker'n a flash of lightning through a gooseberry bush." I poked a flour-covered finger on the pretty prairie dress she was wearing, leaving a thick white circle. "You just see ary I don't row him up Salt River afore he's many more days older."

As far as I was concerned that ended the conversation, if you want to call it that. I still had some baking to do and if you don't knead that dough just right . . . well, sometimes it don't turn out to be what you want it to. Trouble was I was finding it hard to concentrate on what I was doing because the girl was still there. Silent, but still there.

"Oh, I'm supposed to remind you that the picnic is Sunday," she said after a while. It surprised the hell out of me to hear her say that, but she had that beam about her the way a woman gets when she's feeling good about something, and Margaret Dawson was definitely feeling good about the picnic. I'd all but forgotten about it, but now that she mentioned it I was curious as to what was going on.

"You mean Dennison asked you and you actually accepted? After what went on yesterday?" Surprised wasn't anywhere close to describing what I was thinking just then. Hell, if she'd accepted Dennison's invite after what he set her up for, why she must be as addle-brained as the boy! Why, they must be—

"Wait a minute," I said, squinting at her. "Is there something I'm missing here?"

"Well, uh," she stuttered, not even the collar of her dress hiding the pink that was turning to red as it crept up her neck, "Kate was here yesterday." She spit it out, wanting to get it over with as quickly as possible. But once she did the smile returned to her face. "She's really a nice lady, Dallas. She knows so much and I like her and she was really helpful with—"

The red was crawling up her neck again as she took on the look of a rabbit who'd just discovered a couple of hungry wolves and was ready to take flight. She'd shut up before spilling all the beans, but I had a notion I knew what she was talking about.

"She helped you with that meal, didn't she?" Somehow it

had all looked too easy. Thinking back now, I knew it was. She'd looked too composed, too . . . female! You don't work at a meal and not get sweated up or even get your lily-white hands dirty. No, sir, not if you're feeding the Chisum crew.

"Well, I did have a little help," she said nervously.

"Sounds like you're forgetting what my discussion with Sonny was last night." When she looked down at the floor in what I knew was shame, I lifted her chin back up so she faced me when I said, "I don't like liars, remember?"

"I had a lot of help." She said it softly, tears welling up in those big brown eyes. Why do they do it? Why do they act like you've stolen the very last thing of value they have on earth when all you've really done is bruised their feelings. Make you out to be one of those dime novel villains every time, they do. Horse apples!

"Well, don't let it happen again." Now I was the one not speaking all that loud, likely because I didn't want anyone to hear what I'd said. And it's a good thing the boys weren't around, for I'd never have lived down what happened next.

"Oh, Dallas, you're wonderful!" she said, and was suddenly throwing her arms around my neck, hugging me. And just between you and me, hoss, if my hands hadn't been so taken with what I was working on, why, I might just've given her a hug back. But that might not have been too healthful either.

"You get along now, girl. As for the picnic, I doubt I'll make it. Too much work to do. Yup, way too much." I was looking past her when I said it. "Besides, Kate likes young 'uns like you and Dennison, there."

At that last her eyes flew open and she turned around to see Dennison standing in the doorway, a sour, betrayed look on his face. Likely he was thinking the few friends he'd made had deserted him and now the woman he loved was doing the same.

"Woodrow, I was just . . ." The words trailed off as she realized they were hopeless. She looked at me, then Dennison, then back at me, searching for help. But when she gave a second glance, Sonny was gone. The helpless look about her said she was wanting me to go back there and explain to Dennison what had taken place, or hadn't taken place. I shook my head.

"I go back there now, missy, the two of us are gonna tangle and there won't be nothing good comes from it. Hell," I scoffed, "there's no way he's gonna believe anything I say now anyway."

In what must've been pure desperation, she spun around and headed for the back door, lifting her skirts just enough as she made her way so I'd see how pretty her ankles were. Right pretty is what they were.

I'd wasted enough time and went back to work, only half-listening to the conversation going on outside my shack. When I heard her crying, I glanced out the window to see if she'd head straight for the main house or stop dead in her tracks and head back to my cookshack to do something foolish and disrupt my day even more. Well, friend, she stopped all right, and I have to admit that for a second there I was wondering if she hadn't lifted one of my cleavers and was about to pull it out of the folds of that prairie skirt. But she didn't.

Instead the red came to her face and I swear she looked as if she was going to bust a vein in her neck. She hadn't gone but forty feet before stopping and was now lifting the skirt to reveal more than just an ankle, and I'll be the first to admit that it was the calf of her leg I was staring at. But not Margaret Dawson, no, sir. It was the clump that had become attached to her foot that she was staring at, and the more she stared the redder her face got. You see, it's all over the place and a man, well, a man gets used to it. But a woman's got to watch where she's going, even when she's madder than hell, because when it gets on that gussied-up

footwear . . . well, it's not too pleasant. And so far this
hadn't turned out to be such a good day for Margaret Dawson. Fact is, she was catching on as fast as the Dennison boy.
She dropped her skirts, took a step or two forward and
glanced back at the impression her tiny foot had made in
the ground. Slowly, she looked to the heavens and took a
deep breath.

"HORSE APPLES!"

I don't know whether she knew that was what she'd
stepped in or was just picking up one of my phrases, but I'll
guarantee you one thing, hoss. As funny as it might have
seemed, there wasn't a man who heard her who so much as
chuckled as she stalked off toward the main house. Can't
say as I blame them much.

Hell, she might still have had a cleaver in those folds!

Margaret Dawson had pretty much regained her composure by that evening. Of course, no one asked her why
she'd gone from that fancy dress to a pair of jeans, a man's
shirt and a pair of faded old Indian moccasins.

"Dressiest thing I ever did see in those beat-up old
things," Uncle John said, taking notice of how Margaret
had turned up the cuffs of her jeans, showing more than
just a mite of ankle. Naturally, he didn't say it until Sallie
and Margaret had retreated inside and we were alone on
the veranda. It was almost as if things were going back to
normal.

"I'll say."

John lit that corn cob pipe of his while I looked out
toward the horizon. There was a time when John and I
could spend a peaceful evening taking in the same old
sunset, knowing that there wasn't nothing the same about
it at all, because each day left us looking at it from just a
hair's different angle. But in the past year I couldn't recall
all that much peace in Lincoln County. And after John
Tunstall had been killed a short time back, well, all hell had

been breaking loose. So when I say it felt like things were almost back to normal, I reckon I was dreaming, and even that got disrupted that night.

"By the way, Dallas," John said in that formal kind of voice he tried to develop but never could, "I've been meaning to talk to you."

"That so." He was dealing the cards so I figured I'd let him play them out.

"Yes." He paused, squinted over at me and drew on his pipe, making sure what he said was right. "I hear Kate's gonna have a picnic of sorts Sunday." When I didn't respond, he eyed me a bit more suspiciously. "I also hear you ain't going."

"You was anyone else, John, I'd say you had ears the size of one of them circus elephants," I said, which, in a round-about way, was exactly what I did say.

"Well, now, as I recollect it was Kate who told me about the picnic and Miss Margaret who mentioned that you'd uninvited yourself. Nope," he said, taking a pull on that pipe, "big ears didn't have nothing to do with it. Of course, Miss Margaret told me all of that while she was crying her eyes out."

"Personally, I don't see how that girl's gonna get the Dennison boy to go with her," I said. "That boy's 'bout as mule headed as you can get." I thought I heard Uncle John mumble something about it reminding him of me, but passed it off.

"Oh, he's going, all right," he replied, "mule-headed or not. You can bet on that, Dallas." He was the one giving me a case of the suspicions now. "You see, after Miss Margaret got through with all that crying, I got hold of your young helper and persuaded him to take the young lady on the picnic."

Now, that surprised me. Hell, all I'd been able to do was get the bare minimum out of the boy all day, workwise. "That I'd like to hear."

"Oh, it was simple." It was getting darker as the sun disappeared into the horizon, but I'd been with John Chisum too long not to spot a hint of mischief in those eyes as he continued. "I told him if he didn't take Margaret and act proper, I was gonna break his neck. Now I'm telling you the same thing."

I couldn't tell whether he was joshing me or serious, but even when you get to be a couple of old bastards like John and me you take a certain amount of respect into consideration when one of us says something to the other. Only trouble now was that I had the feeling I was being set up for an ambush. These civilized folks would call what John was doing matchmaking, but to me it's nothing more than bushwacking!

"Like I told the girl, John, there's an awful lot of—"

"Horse apples. A lot of horse apples is what it is." As serious as he was trying to be, we both broke out in subdued chuckles over the word, remembering the Dawson girl's curse to the gods earlier in the day. When he got it under control he gave me the kind of look a good friend will give you and I knew he meant it when he said, "Go, Dallas. You go and enjoy yourself. It's been a long time and you deserve it."

"But, John—"

"She said it meant a lot to her, Dallas. I'd hate to see her get disappointed."

What could I say? What could I do but accept? I knew the sincerity of the man next to me, still, it ired me to be forced into going this way.

"Horse apples!" I said in exasperation as I rose to my feet.

"I heard that!" came the stern admonition of Margaret Dawson inside.

"Yes ma'am," I replied, but as John and I parted I wondered if the young girl would ever live it down.

CHAPTER TWELVE

There is a place north of Lincoln called Capitan Gap. It's up there near the Jicarilla Mountains, has water and a wooded area and is a generally nice place to be alone. Kate and I had been there before a time or two and I thought I'd take her there again. That entailed riding into Lincoln to get Kate. She might have been preparing all that chicken, but I had a lot of preparing to do my own self before I left. So while the youngsters were getting all prettied up for this affair, I set about making a few things the lads on the crew would likely steal into my kitchen and snatch up anyway once I was gone. It wasn't but a couple hours after breakfast that I found Lang and let him know what I'd done.

"I leave you birds alone for any length of time and I know that when I get back I'm gonna find this kitchen plundered worse than Georgia after Sherman marched through it," I told him, pointing out what I'd made for them.

"All right, cookie," he said. Except for the times he was trying to pry some more food or a favor out of me, it was the first time I'd seen him genuinely smile at me. "I'll tell the boys."

"One other thing, Lang," I cautioned as he readied to leave.

"Yeah."

"When I get back the only things that better be gone are what I've laid out here and the six-shooter coffee in that pot." I threw him a glance that said that this comment was all business. "You just tell the boys that ary I find anything missing, I'll be fixing up Rocky Mountain oysters for the next meal, *and the contents won't come from anything walking around on four legs at your roundup.*"

Tom Lang gulped hard at that last sentence. "I think the boys'll get the drift of what you're saying."

"Is that another one of your world-famous recipes?"

I turned around to see Margaret Dawson looking as beautiful as the day she'd come to the ranch. It wasn't anything fancy she was wearing, you understand, just plain old gingham that you'd see on most women out here. Or maybe it was the woman wearing it. That's usually how it is.

"Well, now, ain't you the picture to be painted," I said. I wasn't about to make any comment on the riding boots she wore instead of the fancy footwear she'd had on the other day. After what I'd seen and heard a couple of days back, this woman might start a war of her own if she got riled enough. And that definitely was on the agenda today.

"Thank you." I must've been the only one to say it to her so far for she beamed all over. "Rocky Mountain oysters?"

"Sure, it's—" Before I could say any more I remembered what they were and said, "It's just a dish we serve out here. Nothing really." How do you explain to a virginal eighteen-year-old girl that Rocky Mountain oysters is bull's balls? Tell me that! So I just passed them off as nothing, even if they were a bit of a delicacy out here. Like I said, I wasn't about to start another war.

"Don't you think we'd better get started?" It was the first time Dennison had spoken to me in three days, other than replying yes or no or nodding his head when I'd given him instructions. But he was still as dour as he had been then, which made Kate and Margaret the only ones who were enthusiastic about this picnic.

"Horses ready?" I asked, untying my apron, but the boy's only response was a nod and a mumble.

Actually, I wasn't feeling all that fired up about this get-together either, and I reckon it showed as we set out for Lincoln at an easy pace on our mounts.

"Is there something wrong, Dallas?" the girl asked after we'd ridden in silence awhile. Now, friend, hedging the truth is the kind of thing you do when a pretty young girl asks you about Rocky Mountain oysters. Other than that . . . well, I've never been too good at it.

"I reckon it's this whole shindig idea."

Margaret gave me one of those sly, womanly looks. "You're not going to tell me you don't like Kate, are you?"

"Oh no, I like Kate fine. It's just that I'm gonna take some funning about this once I get back."

"Whatever for?" The idea truly puzzled her.

"Don't know as I could explain that to you right, ma'am."

After a short silence, she looked my way and said, "I may be tougher than you think, Dallas. Why don't you try me?" The confidence in her voice had transferred itself to her face now, reminding me of Kate some.

"Well, ma'am, it's like this," I said, trying hard to think of a way to say what was on my mind without hurting anyone's feelings and knowing I couldn't. "You live in this land as long as I have and you get to know a lot about it. And its people. Yes, ma'am.

"A lot of Easterners come out here a-figuring we're the sort they've read about in them dime novels, and that just ain't so. Get 'em a set of clothes that makes 'em look like one of the dime novel characters they been reading 'bout, but can't for the life of 'em understand why they get called Monkey Ward cowboys.

"Now, you take Dennison here." I was riding in the center, one of them on either side of me. "Fancies hisself to be a cowhand." Margaret leaned forward in the saddle, looking past me at Sonny. "You sure you want to hear this, missy?"

"Yes, of course." More confidence and smile.

"Them strange birds they call accountants." I paused.

"And bankers, them too." Margaret Dawson frowned at me in uncertainty. When I said, "Roll their sleeves," it only added to the confusion on her face. "One of 'em rolls his sleeves so's he can tally the books and see ary he don't make as much a mess with the feather and ink as he does with the books; other one figures it'll make him look less like a river rat gambler ary he rolls his sleeves, but you can bet that if he ain't palming cards out his sleeve, he's slipping a bill or two in his pocket while you ain't looking."

"Get to the point," Sonny said. Wasn't even calling me by my name anymore. Developing a temper too, it seemed, at least from the tone of his voice now. Well, I could be testy too, friend.

"The point is, *children*," I said, emphasizing that last word and looking as crusty as any badge dodger could, "that oncet you been out here long enough to know the lizards by their first names, you also know that no cowhand ever *rolled* his sleeves to go to work, packed him a *picnic* lunch or said 'Good gracious' when he meant *goddamn*."

"Oh," the girl said in that way a female does when she's bit off a mite more of this man's world than she figured she could handle, and would rather go back to looking coy and shy again. As for Dennison, well, let's just say that when I gave him a glance he didn't have those sleeves of his rolled up anymore.

"That, children, is what the crew is gonna rib me about."

Then I let that old mustang feel my heels and lit out, leaving the two of them behind.

"My, but you're here early," Kate said when I arrived, Dennison and the girl not far behind. She was her usual pleasant as could be self and I could tell she was looking forward to this outing.

"Let the horses have their heads," I said as Sonny and Margaret dismounted. "Besides, these two couldn't wait to get here to see you," I added, glancing over my shoulder at the pair. It didn't take much to see that Margaret Dawson was, indeed, in high spirits over seeing the older woman again. I got the impression that Dennison had even taken a liking to her, the way he smiled and gave her a tip of the hat. It was when he threw a sideward glance at me that I knew it wasn't over between me and this pilgrim.

"Seems to me I smell something familiar," I said, knowing full well it was the chicken Kate had promised.

"He's been trying to get my recipe for over a year now," Kate said, addressing the younger couple. She had a way of letting those around her know what her intentions were about the two of us, this woman. "Maybe someday I'll let him know . . . if he has anything worth trading for it." The way she looked at me and the way she said that last, why, she was letting these youngsters and anyone else who happened to be listening know that she'd set her cap for me, and I don't mind telling you that it made me nervous!

But before I had a chance to think anymore about it Kate was giving orders to Dennison and me, telling us where the vittles were and how she wanted them loaded in her buckboard as she and the Dawson girl disappeared from sight. The tension I'd felt all morning was still there between us. Maybe it was because Uncle John had forced the both of us to come, but mostly it was the thought that no matter how much good behavior I tried to be on Sonny might ruin the whole day. It was almost as if he were hunting trouble just to prove himself again to whoever it was he figured it was he had to prove himself to.

When we left for Capitan Gap I told Sonny to tie his and Margaret's mounts to the rear of the buckboard and join the girl on the ride. He was back to his nodding and grumbling by then. Kate had her usual jeans and work shirt on, which must've seemed second nature to most of us who knew her.

"Someday I'm gonna make my way down to Taos and get you one of them pretty dresses like the *señoritas* wear," I said, as we rode some distance behind the buckboard. I thought it would make her happy but the look on her face was a cross between horror and fear and I couldn't understand why. "Did I say something—"

"No," she said slowly, regaining her composure. "I just never was much for dressing up, I guess." The weak smile told me it was a lie, but I knew better than to go into the why and wherefore of it. This was supposed to be a day we could all enjoy and I didn't want to ruin it any more than I had to.

It's times like that you get to wondering if the Maker didn't invent weather just so a body would have a conversation piece when the words inside you dry up. I said nothing more about dressing up on the way to Capitan Gap, but in the back of my mind was the lingering thought that like it or not I'd struck a nerve in Kate Rogers' past and I honest to God didn't want to hurt her.

You'd think that in a land as barren as the New Mexico Territory is in places it would be hard to find good foliage and shrubs and such, but it's not. Whether you call it advanced growth or windbreaks or anything in between, the offshoots of the numerous mountain ranges will offer you a decent amount of trees to have a picnic lunch under . . . if you know the right place to look. Kate and I knew the right place.

Even for being April the days could get fearsome hot if Mother Nature took a mind to it, and a shaded spot in a cool breeze was what all of us needed after that ride.

Kate is right, someday I'm going to get that recipe for her chicken from her. It was so good that Dennison wasn't paying much attention at all, but I thought I saw a playful glance between Kate and Margaret Dawson while we were eating. It was the kind of look that's supposed to be what a man'll think is anngelliferous but a woman knows to be devious. Now, friend, I wouldn't say that Mama was the only woman I've ever been around in my life, but these two were up to something . . . I just wasn't sure what it was.

"How do you like being a cook's helper?" Kate asked innocently enough as we finished the meal. I gave her a look of my own when she said it, but there wasn't anything devious about my meaning; I was curious as to whether or not she'd taken to playing with matches around a stick of dynamite of late just to amuse herself or if senility was creeping in on her as much as I felt like it was on me?

"Not one bit!" I do believe he would've swallowed one of those chicken bones whole before spitting it out as hard as he did those words. At least the boy wasn't playing any games at it.

"Mama didn't teach you much in the way of manners, did she." It was a comment, not a question. "Never talk with your mouth full, son. It's bad manners."

"What the hell are you talking about?" he asked, looking about as confused as the two women by my statement.

"You've already stuck your foot in your mouth more'n oncet, Sonny. I don't think it's big enough to fit a third boot into." I paused, squinted a challenging eye at him. "Or is it?"

Maybe that run-in I'd had with him a few days back after Blazer's Mill held his reins back as far as that quick temper he was developing. Or maybe it was because of the women present that he didn't reply. Hell, maybe he was just wanting to take me out back of my own shed and have at me, I don't know. But all he did was glare at me for what was likely the longest five seconds of that day for the four of us.

"Actually, the cook is one of the most important people in camp, Sonny," Kate said in a cheerful way. Good thing, too, for that boy stared any harder and his eyeballs would've fallen out. "Why, even the boss has a good respect for the cook."

"I'll say," Margaret said, joining in. "Why, Mr. Chisum has a whole lot of respect for Dallas." At first it sounded good to her, but she sort of blushed with embarrassment when she saw the half-sad, half-mad look in Dennison's eyes. And it didn't take all the educating in the world to know the boy was thinking that although big John Chisum might have thought the world of me, he didn't think an awful lot of this tenderfoot who'd entered his life.

"You ask any of the crew that works for Chisum or any of the other ranchers in the territory, Sonny, and you find that as much as they complain about him, nearly all of them have a great deal of respect for the range cook." Kate was laying it on pretty thick. What she was saying was all true, of course, but a man didn't hear his work or his job described as being all that good out here—not often. "He'll settle a bet, or even hold the money for one. He holds a cowhand's money for him so he won't lose it out on the range while he's working. He'll listen to your complaints or your confessions if you like, and he'll doctor up man or beast with some of the strangest and most god-awful concoctions ever made." She paused a moment, glancing my way, a familiar smile now on her face. "And if he's worth his salt, his stories will be as good as his food." Then, with that same self-assured smile, she added a wink at Dennison. "Don't count yourself out, Woodrow. Being a cook isn't as glamorous as having the reputation of Wild Bill Hickok or Buffalo Bill, but it's just as necessary as being the town marshal out here."

Kate has a way of terminating a conversation by getting started doing something else. It was one of the things that made me feel a bit uneasy with her. After she'd spoken her piece, she and the Dawson girl began cleaning up the remains of the chicken she'd cooked, which was now mostly bones that looked like they'd been stripped down to nothing by someone who hadn't eaten in a month. That left Dennison and me to wile away ten minutes of time without biting one another's head off, and I do believe that we both of us tried hard for neither of us did much speaking while the ladies went about their business.

"Woodrow, could you show me some of the trees over there?" Margaret asked the man she'd come with, pointing off in a direction that seemed almost as if it was planned that way. The boy might have been somewhere between sullen and contemplative by the looks of him, but he grudgingly went with her. It wasn't but a minute later that Kate was encircling her arm in mine as I watched the two youngsters disappear into the trees.

"Come on." Kate tugged at my arm. No what do you think of taking a walk, or so much as a by your leave, not from Kate. Like I say, the woman has a mind of her own. And if Dennison and the girl were heading east, it was west that she was pulling me toward. When I frowned at her, resisting for a moment, she said, "Well, do you want to take a walk or not?"

"Not until I get an answer to something." Maybe she was feeling full of play and fun, but I was a bit confused.

"All right. What is it?" She was going to have her way, she knew that, and if I got crusty . . . well, it was only a minor setback. She was so sure of herself, in fact, that even as she spoke she had me walking with her into the trees, and I can't say as I gave her much of an argument on it.

"What was all that giggling that went on back there between you and that Dawson girl? Something tells me it's got something to do with this little excursion into the wilderness."

We walked maybe a hundred feet in silence before coming to a small clearing to one side. It wasn't big by any means; hell, my cookshack was bigger than this. But it was where Kate had led me and when she took a seat on the ground she had a hold of my hand, making sure that I took a place next to her.

"You men aren't the only ones who make bets, Dallas," she said, still smiling in that mischievous way she had about her. And you can bet I was wondering what she had up her sleeve. "I told Margaret that if she could keep young Woodrow's interest for an hour while I talked to you I'd give her the recipe to that chicken we just ate."

Me a cook and she was giving that recipe to a young lady who I seriously doubted could boil water without burning it! The thought rushed through my mind in a flash, but before I could blurt it out, she was leaning over—as awkward a manner as it was—and kissing me. It wasn't a long kiss, just a short one, but you can bet the farm she had taken my mind off Margaret Dawson, Woodrow Dennison, chicken and recipes. Me, shocked? Let's just say that I've had less surprise from an Apache war party.

"You know, Dallas, if you keep that petrified look on your face, I'm going to start thinking I was right."

"Huh?" I couldn't move, just sat there looking at her, wondering when they were going to plant me up north in that forest Bridger called petrified.

"I'm going to start thinking that you're the only one who doesn't know I'm in love with you." She leaned over again, but this time the kiss was a soft, lingering one as a strange feeling came over me, one that brought me back to the present and reminded me of long ago at the same time—if that's possible.

"Well, I . . ." I wasn't sure what I thought. Sure I'd known Kate for a couple of years, admiring her more than most women I'd met because she was self-sufficient, independent. It was something you took for granted in most men, but was really an accomplishment for a woman out here. For that she had my own respect and that of most others who dealt with her. But to be in *love?* I had feelings for the woman, to be sure, but at the moment they were all mixed up. Or maybe that's the way they're supposed to be at times like these.

"I didn't know," was all I could finally muster, still not sure what was taking place.

"Yes you did." The smile was half-gone now, replaced by a serious tone. "There are times I see it in your eyes, Dallas. Yes, you knew.

"I doubt that you'll ever see me wearing the dresses your Taos *señoritas* do." Like I said, she had a way of changing the subject whenever she wanted to, only I had the notion this wasn't really a change of subject as much as it was an extension of one. The subject, of course, being Kate Rogers and Dallas Haywood. "It's not that I don't want to either. Believe it or not, I was once very good at dancing." I still wasn't sure what was going on but one thing I did know and that was that even though she was looking at me while she spoke, it was the past she was seeing now. When she began to take off her boots I offered to lend a hand but she insisted she'd done it by herself for some time now.

"Fixing to get comfortable, are you?"

"I don't think you'll feel comfortable about this, Dallas." When the boots were off she turned up the cuffs of her jeans and rolled down the white wool socks covering her feet. "That's why I won't wear a dress."

"Jesus, Mary and Joseph!" If her kissing me was a shock, what I now saw could have knocked me dead. She was right, there was something extremely uncomfortable about what I saw.

The scars on both legs extended up most of the calf. They were the thick, ugly kind that take one hell of a long time to heal and will be with you for a lifetime. Staring at them will turn your stomach and I reckon Kate knew that, for when she saw the look on my face she immediately pulled the socks back up and rolled the pants legs down. When I looked up at her, the laughter was gone, in its place a look of fear and harsh remembrance.

"Dan and I had a small ranch in west Texas for a while, one we made a decent living at, believe it or not." I knew she was widowed but had never heard anything about her past, not even from the women in the area who were

known to sniff out information like that. I'd gone to the
Montano store a couple of years back and there she was and
that was that. "Unfortunately, there are just as many
greedy people in this world as there are good ones and the
greedy ones want it all. Maybe that's why I wasn't too
appalled at Billy killing Sheriff Brady.

"They came one afternoon, a half dozen of them. I guess
they thought they were toughs, but Dan didn't scare and
neither did I and when one of them went for his gun, Dan
shot him out of the saddle.

"They said they'd be back." She looked at me with sor-
rowful eyes, just a glance before they were trained once
again on the trees and branches and leaves surrounding us
as though searching for one glimmer of light in all of that
dark green and brown.

"Look, Kate," I mumbled awkwardly, not knowing what
it was I should be saying or doing, "you don't have to tell
me. Why, shoot, it ain't none of my business, and—"

"No," she replied, still staring at the foliage, "it's about
time I told someone. I've been reliving it every night for
four years now. Maybe if I tell it all, I'll finally have some
peace of mind." She sniffled and I figured the end wasn't
far away, and that meant neither were the tears.

"They wanted it all, but they made the mistake of coming just at sundown when you can silhouette them against
the fading light. Dan shot two more out of the saddle while
one of them set the house on fire. They didn't think a
woman would fight back, but I did. I killed one of them just
outside the front door before another shot me and left me
for dead." She undid the top three buttons of her shirt,
pulling the left side down enough to reveal the scar that
only a bullet wound would leave high in the chest.

She went on to tell of how she had run out the door,
stumbled over the dead body of the man she had shot and
passed out when she hit the ground. They told her later
that someone had seen the fire from a distance and come as

fast as they could. If it hadn't been for that she might have died. The only thing that had saved her from losing her feet had been the fact that she had been wearing boots then. Otherwise . . . well, she didn't want to think about it and neither did I.

She was strong, this woman, for she'd gone through it all, relived the whole story and not yet shed a tear. Looked like she was ready to start bawling all the way through it, but hadn't yet. Me, I didn't know what to say.

"When I came to Lincoln I had nothing but bitter memories." Her voice was much softer, lower now and I knew it was me she was speaking to as she turned to me, not the past, not anyone else. "Then you started coming into Montano's and you reminded me so much of Dan. So kind and gentle."

"Me?" Now, that threw me for a loop. Hell, all I could ever recall being described as was a crusty old biscuit shooter at best. Me, gentle and kind? Are you joshing me, grandmother?

"There's so much about you, but . . ." A single tear rolled down a cheek as the sentence trailed off. She turned her whole body toward me and I was suddenly aware of those undone buttons on her shirt and how healthy Kate Rogers was.

"You'd better button that shirt up, Kate, or you're likely to catch some of that breeze." Well, what did you think I was going to say! I'm no ladies' man!

"Don't you see, Dallas, you're the only one who doesn't know that I love you." For one instant I thought I saw something in her eyes, something that told me she was as scared as I was about all of this. Then another tear rolled down a cheek and she was kissing me, except it was more like tackling me as she did.

I didn't find myself resisting her this time and kissed her back and to hell with those buttons. Maybe it was love.

Maybe I didn't even know it. Hell, I don't know. From there on in it got sort of private, if you know what I mean.

Fact is, all you have to know is that that afternoon Kate Rogers made her intentions known.

And so did I.

CHAPTER THIRTEEN

It was late that night when we got back to the Jinglebob, but I'll say one thing—I was one hell of a lot more conversational than I had been when we left that morning. I reckon that's why it did not strike me until the next morning that on the way back, as good as I was feeling, the two youngsters had been downright solemn.

"Say, what happened with you two yesterday?" I asked Sonny when he came in the next morning. Me, I was still sounding conversational, still remembering the time Kate and I had spent together. Dennison, well, friend, he wasn't as mean or loud-mouthed as he had been the day before, but he damn sure wasn't a happy man by any means.

"Nothing," was his reply. "Nothing happened." Then he went back to preparing some batter I'd started on for flapjacks. Oh, something had happened all right. This lad just wasn't talking about it.

"Doesn't look like the boys did too much damage to your castle," Tom Lang said, entering not long afterward and giving the place a once-over. So far everyone was in a reasonably good mood except Dennison.

"No, but I'd like to know who the damn fool was that tried using the same grounds to make a second pot of coffee," I said, eyeing the foreman with suspicion. "That stuff was weaker'n the knees on a newborn colt." I reckon in one way cooks are like dentists: Everyone figures they're grouchy and vengeful. And if that was part of Tom Lang's thinking I sure didn't want to disappoint him, even if I was in a better mood than most days.

"Listen," Lang said, ignoring my remark, "we're going to be going out a ways today. How about some of that jerked beef you've got hid somewhere around here? Piece or two ought to tide the crew over till we get back this afternoon."

"You bet. Speaking of listening, Lang, you'd better tell them loafers to fall to right quick." I jerked a thumb over my shoulder at Sonny, who already had a half stack and was working on some more. "They don't call 'em hot cakes for nothing, you know." Lang smiled as he left, but I knew that as long as I had sorghum to cover them, the crew would eat damn near any kind of flapjack I made.

You'd have thought these birds hadn't seen food in a week's time and were about to pass out from the smell coming from my cookshack as they filed in and took a seat.

"Feel like chawing this morning?" I asked as I set two plates of hot cakes on the table and saw them disappear in record time. Some folks, like Dennison, who gave me a strange look, get the idea that we're talking about talking or chewing tobacco or such when you ask if a fellow feels like chawing, when all we're asking is if he's hungry.

These boys were hungry.

"Say, cookie, how'd that *picnic* of yours go?" one of them asked when he decided to give his jaw a rest from all that chewing. "You get any more fancy recipes out of that widow lady?"

The red started crawling up my neck, the way it does on you when someone says something that gets close to what you know and they aren't supposed to. But I put it to good use and put on a show of what they call righteous indignation; after all, a man ought to learn something from watching a politician if only that he's a liar and knows how to put it to good use.

"Don't josh me, boy," I said. "Kate Rogers serves up the best fried chicken I ever did taste, but I doubt she'll ever give me the recipe for it. Shoot, she went and give it to Miss

Margaret instead!" There were a couple of chuckles among them. "Looks like I'm gonna have to court Miss Margaret now." That gave them a good belly laugh, knowing that I'd be after the woman for her recipes more than romance.

"You can have her." It was the first time Dennison had spoken up during the meal, and I had a notion I knew what was bothering him. Something had gone sour between him and the girl yesterday.

"What's wrong with him?" one of the hands asked.

I glanced over my shoulder, back at the cowhand. "He ain't mixing the medicine too awful well this morning."

"And what in the hell's THAT supposed to mean!" the boy yelled out, throwing the spatula down on the floor like some spoiled kid. Spoiled or not, you don't treat my equipment like Dennison just had, not even if you're the President!

"It means you've got a helluva lot better handle on that spatula than you do on whatever's eating at your insides," I said as the nearest fist shot out at him, a stubby finger poking him in the chest. "And if there ain't nothing left of that spatula handle when you pick it up, Sonny, I'm gonna use you for an example of how we used to declaw mountain lions up in the Rockies."

"All right, boys, let's clear out of here," Tom Lang said.

"But, boss, there's a fight brewing," one man said, obviously wanting to stick around to see what happened.

"Don't doubt it one bit, Shorty, but it's *their* fight, not ours. Now, come on, move it out of here. We got work to do." When the crew had left, Dennison and I were standing there staring at one another, each waiting for the other to move. "When you get him stood in the corner, Dallas, I'd appreciate that jerked beef."

I don't know if Dennison figured he'd won that staring contest or not, but I knew there was more to be done than just look at one another and see whose eyeballs would fall out first. I got a possibles sack from the corner and handed it to Lang, who then had the good sense to leave.

"Come on, pilgrim," I growled, grabbing a smaller pot of coffee as I headed out the side door for the main house.

"Morning, Dallas," Uncle John said from the veranda. Without a word I walked past him, set the coffeepot down on the table inside, poured a cup and took it back out to Chisum.

"Horse apples," I said, thrusting the steaming cup at him. I would have said a few more colorful words, but you never can tell when a woman'll appear in a house like that, especially when there's two of them.

"What now?" he asked, heaving a sigh as though he knew what I'd say next.

"I'll tell you what now!" I looked at Dennison, who still had that madder than hell face he'd developed in the last few minutes. "I've had enough of him, that's what!"

"Looks like he's feeling the same way 'bout you," the big rancher said, calmly taking a pull on his coffee. "Ain't nothing better'n fresh brewed coffee." He paused for a second, a thought crossing his mind as a smile came to his face. "Well, almost nothing."

"Did you hear what I said?"

"Yup," he replied, gulping the rest of the coffee. "Said you'd had enough of him. I need some more coffee, myself." He headed back into the house, followed by Dennison and me. "What seems to be the problem?" he finally said, after pouring more coffee.

"I want him out of my kitchen! That's what the problem is!" Now, friend, I'm not a yeller like some are, but when I get mad you know about it, and John Chisum was about to find out how mad that was. "He ain't caused nothing but trouble since he's been here! Why, my aunt Martha over to Houston moves faster'n this squirt does!"

"Aunt Martha." He said it calmly, trying to picture her in

his mind. "Isn't she the one you said was pushing a hundred or so?"

"Betcher"—I stopped right quick as I caught sight of Sallie and Margaret coming down the hallway and swiped the hat off my head. "Morning, ladies," I said in as civil a tone as I could manage. Once that was taken care of, I was looking up at Big John Chisum and it was all business again. "I've spent more time this past week trying to get him out of trouble than I have tending to the cooking. The Kid put it in his mind he could be some kind of *pistolero* in no time. On top of that he's moon-eyed and pushy and looking for trouble . . . as if he don't get in enough on his own." I was about to gather another breath of air when Uncle John broke in.

"That true, Mr. Dennison? You looking for trouble, are you?" There was enough trouble around these days without having to go out of your way to look for it and Uncle John wouldn't allow any on the Jinglebob, that much I knew.

"Never mind, Mr. Chisum," Dennison said, the fire in him all but gone now, "I won't bother you any more." He turned to leave, but Chisum had a hold of his arm before he'd gone far and it was a good thing too. Me, I was standing right in that doorway and I can guarantee you I'd have pushed more than a stubby finger into that boy's chest this time.

"You just wait a minute, son. We got us some talking to do. Now, like I was saying—"

"What's the use!" the boy busted out. "I don't understand nothing you say or do. Nobody speaks English out here."

"Are you sure it's as much that we don't speak English as it is that you don't talk Western, son? You just have a seat and think about that a minute." To me he said, "I imagine there's plenty of work to be done."

"That don't never stop, boss." I figured that was my

signal to leave, but as I walked out of the house I found myself being accompanied by Uncle John. When we were out of earshot of the house, he stopped, gave me a hard, concerned look.

"Don't be too hard on him, Dallas. He's new out here. It takes 'em time when they come out like that, you know that as well as I do. Besides, the both of us were his age too a couple of centuries back."

"Might be, John, but you know good and goddamn well that if we'd acted like he has back then we wouldn't have lasted till midday, much less the end of the day!"

He smiled, remembering way back when. "You're probably right, Dallas, you're probably right." Then he headed for the main house.

I set to cleaning the cookshack up, cussing the gods, the earth, what little I knew of the universe, and anything else that came to mind. I was back to working this whole operation by my lonesome and was none too happy about it. To tell the truth, I got to where I was enjoying having the extra help around, had even begun to take a liking to the Dennison boy until he'd gone mean on me. Thinking of that only got me mad all over again and I took to cussing once more.

"I didn't know there were that many swear words in the world." I turned to silently see Margaret Dawson, a bit red in the face and a bit awed by the look of her.

"I thought I told you not to do that to a man." She was a beautiful girl all right but the sight of her didn't do anything for my disposition at the moment. If anything, it maddened me that much more to know I'd been overheard.

"I'm sorry."

"Never apologize. It's a sign of weakness," I said, going back to my work. It flashed through my mind then and I glanced over my shoulder at the girl, giving her my best scowl. "But then, you're a feline, ain't you? Reckon I oughtta expect it."

Before I could resume my duties, she had a pair of raw-hide gloves in her hand and a look on her face that could kill. "I brought my own this morning," she said, giving a wave of the fistful of rawhide and trying to sound tough. Then she was gone and in a matter of seconds I heard the ax falling on deadwood outside. In ten minutes the ax was silent and she was once again standing in the doorway. I reckon she saw my smile when she went to get the dipper for some water. It hit her then as fast as it had me.

"You did that on purpose!" she said in an accusing tone.

"You bet." Hell, I wasn't going to lie to her. "Work this spread yourself and you find out real quick that time is something you don't get much of all to oncet. Insult the intruders hard enough and they either go away or figure they can show you how much they can do their own self." I smiled, winked at her. "I just got me a couple more logs I won't have to cut up."

I wiped my forehead, took the dipper from her hand, found some *agua* and then handed her a full dipper when I was through.

"I'd really like to talk to you, Dallas, if you've got the time," she said after finishing off the water. She was wearing those jeans and a man's shirt this time and when she raised her arm to wipe her forehead I saw that she had actually developed some sweat under it.

"Maybe I'm getting old and senile," I said, scratching the back of my head, "but didn't I just say I didn't have time to palaver with anyone? You want to palaver around here and you'll have to work more than your mouth."

She shrugged, satisfied with my working philosophy. "Seems fair enough." At least she was outgoing and willing to help, where Dennison, for all the nobility he'd started out with in that saloon with Turk Calder, had grown shy or so outspoken he'd become abrasive. There ain't much room for either one of those extremes out here. It's a land of survivors and if you've got enough sand to make a go of it without bragging about everything you do . . . well, you just might make it. But those that were as helpless as the Dennison boy seemed at times or as braggadocious as the likes of Turk Calder, they were the ones who wound up being buzzard bait. I found her something to do in the shack there with me and got back to what I was doing my own self.

"It's Woodrow, I mean Sonny, that I wanted to talk to you about," she said slowly, almost as if she were afraid to bring the subject up. She was on the right trail on that one.

"Less said 'bout him, the better. Boy reminds me of a bullfrog."

"A bullfrog?" She found this somewhat amusing from the curious look that cropped up on her face.

"Yup. All mouth and no"—I caught myself short, knowing at the last minute, just like always, that I was in the presence of a woman. "Well, you know what I mean."

She smiled, although this time it was only her cheeks that blushed. "Yes, I think I do."

Whatever it was she was going to discuss about Dennison didn't get said because the next thing I knew the lad was standing in the doorway. And somehow I had the feeling that was a surprise to all three of us.

"What do I do next?" His tone of voice was considerably more respectful than earlier this morning.

"Next?"

"Mr. Chisum said for me to do as you say and keep my mouth shut. Now, what do I do next?"

He might have been talking to me but he was looking at the girl. Whatever had happened on the other side of that picnic ground the day before looked to be unhappening now, as the girl began to smile and return his cow-eyed gaze.

"Love is gonna be the ruin of me yet." I do believe if I hadn't said it in the crusty old way they were getting used to me speaking, why, they wouldn't have heard me at all.

But when I had their attention I didn't waste any time. "Sonny, get out back and go after that side of meat ary it ain't got tiresome and left already." Without a word he walked off. "Missy, you want to be helpful you either get on back to the house and do whatever it is you and Miss Sallie do all day, or grab that ax handle." I gave a glance at the cowhide covering her hands. "I hate to see a good pair of gloves go to waste."

That's what you get for letting folks know where you stand, especially if it's on their foot and they want to get out from under you. Do just about anything to get out of your sight once they know you mean business, and both of these youngsters had done just that. Dennison was soon out back hacking away at the beef like I told him, and Margaret, pretty as she was, was working up a man-like sweat at the woodpile.

Uncle John had apparently given the Dennison boy a talking to that set him straight about what it was he was to do on the Jinglebob. I now had both of these youngsters working out of each other's sight and was getting my own work done to boot. Hell, I was even thinking back to Kate and how good I'd felt that morning when I got up. You'd have thought all was right with the world and all that poetic stuff.

No such luck.

It wasn't but half an hour later that I heard the ax stop falling on that deadwood outside and figured Margaret Dawson had had her fill of man's work for the day and left. But that wasn't it. I thought I heard her moan before she said, "Stop it!" and started cussing to myself as I made my way to the door.

"What in the hell is"—I started to say but never did finish it. What happened next took place pretty fast.

Tom Lang was standing by the woodpile, holding Margaret Dawson by the shoulders and kissing her, and from the way she was squirming I knew she didn't find it too awful pleasurable. I took a step forward but got knocked back by Dennison, who was flying past me like an Apache looking for cover in the barren desert. He tackled both Lang and the girl, all three of them going to the ground in a thud. The girl had the good sense to roll away while she could, but Dennison still didn't know an awful lot about rough and tumble fighting. You don't throw roundhouse punches while you're on the ground with your opponent unless you're sitting on top of him and in a position to beat the living hell out of him and take your time doing it. Sonny raised his fist and it was all the warning Lang needed as his own fist shot out at the boy, knocking him away.

The boy was semiconscious as Lang got to his feet. If they were going to have it out over the girl, then let it be once and for all, I thought, but the foreman must've thought I was going to jump in like I usually did.

"You heard him this morning, Dallas," he said with a voice as hard as the look he gave me, "he said he didn't want her. So I'm taking her." The more he spoke the meaner he sounded, more determined than ever to have his way.

"Now, Tom, you know good and well you ain't taking her." Not that I'd exactly call him my friend, but maybe treating him like it, calling him by his first name, would simmer him down.

It didn't.

"SONNY!" It should've been clear then just who it was that Margaret Dawson cared for or she wouldn't have called out the lad's name when he made the damn fool move of reaching for the ax as he tried to get up. She was fearing for Woodrow Dennison when she sent out that alarm. Something told me that she knew what the outcome would have been had he carried through his act.

Tom Lang could've killed him then and there and claimed self-defense and no jury in the world would have charged him with murder. Hell, Dennison was acting like a desperate man and all of us knew he'd have planted that ax in Lang's side like it was so much deadwood. But just like the gods were making life miserable for me of late—except for that time with Kate—they were also looking over the fools in this world, one of which was Woodrow Dennison. Oh, Tom Lang drew his Colt all right, and he was going to kill Sonny then and there, you could see it in his eyes. And there wasn't any time for me to get my Greener to stop it. But he never did it. No, sir.

The shot came from nowhere, and so did Billy the Kid. The Colt flew out of Lang's fist as the Kid stepped out from around the front of the cookshack. Lang wasn't bleeding anywhere that I could see, more shocked than anything, standing there shaking his hand up and down. I wondered if that accident was because of dumb luck or because the Kid was good. Most likely the latter.

"I wouldn't do that," Billy said as Lang eyed the spot his pistol had fallen at. If he was wanting to kill Sonny just a few seconds before, he was wanting to kill Billy the Kid twice as badly now. He glanced back and forth, from the gun to the Kid, and it was tempting to try. "You want to but you ain't sure, are you, friend?" the Kid said in that cock-sure manner he had at times like these. "Well, you go right ahead if you feel chancy. But I'll guarantee you the last thing you'll see is the ground coming up to hit your face." The Kid hadn't holstered his gun and Lang and I knew he'd be a dead man if he tried it.

"PUT IT AWAY!" The commanding voice came from the veranda and it came from John Chisum as we all turned our attention to him. He had a Winchester up to his shoulder and it was sighted in on the Kid. When nobody moved, he added, "NOW!" No one moved but the Kid as he slowly holstered his pistol.

There ain't no way in hell you'd ever call the man walking toward us then "Uncle John." "Big John" maybe, but there wasn't anything pleasant about the scowl on his face.

I had a grim notion that he wasn't too pleased with any of us. He held the rifle in one hand, waist high, the barrel still pointed in the general direction of Billy the Kid. And I'll tell you, friend, that rifle was plumb making the Kid nervous.

"I could kill you, you know," the Kid said, a bit of his confidence gone. "Even with my gun holstered, I could."

Chisum's face was granite hard and about as mean as I'd seen it in some years. "Don't doubt it a bit, son. But my reflexes would kill you, and truth be known I don't really give a damn at the moment. Now, what the hell's going on?"

"The big man there was about to gun down Sonny," the Kid volunteered.

"I come in to get some more ammunition, Mr. Chisum," the foreman said, picking up his gun, inspecting it and putting away.

"Then how come I found you forcing yourself on Margaret, here!" Sonny said, and there wasn't anything shy about him now.

"You mean *that's* what this is over?" the rancher asked incredulously. "Her?" Like I said, he wasn't pleased with any of us, and Margaret wasn't an exception. He got red and mad and furious as hell in all of ten seconds of silence. But you can bet none of us was about to take a chance on making him any the madder. "Well, you get your ammunition, Lang, and get back on that range where you're supposed to be." Clearly, he didn't believe Tom Lang for a minute, and that got the foreman about as mad as his boss as he stomped off, returning shortly with a possibles sack of what must have been ammunition. "You leave the women alone on this ranch, Lang. You hear me?"

"Yeah, I hear you, *Chisum.*" No "mister," no respect at all in the way he said it as he mounted his horse. "By the way, *Chisum,* the reason I come to get the ammunition is some of the boys spotted a half dozen men cutting steers outta the herd. One of them could've been Turk Calder."

"Well, why didn't you—"

"Something else, *Chisum*. This season's over, I'll be moving on. I never took to working for anyone that come as close as you just did to calling me a liar."

Then he was gone.

"Goddamn it!" Being wrong never helped no man's disposition, especially when he's done it in front of someone else, and Big John Chisum just got madder. "Bonney, you get the hell outta here before I make it open season on wolves." To Sonny he added, "You too. You've run outta chances on this spread, so git."

The boy looked as though he'd been hit in the gut, unsure of what it was he'd done wrong. After brief glances at Chisum, me and the girl, I reckon he figured that the Kid was the only sympathetic one there.

"Let me get a horse, Billy," he finally said. "I'm coming with you."

"You," Chisum said, addressing the girl, "I don't know what I'm gonna do about you." Without waiting for an answer he turned his cussedness toward me. "Well, what are you waiting for, Dallas! Git back to work! It's what I hired you for!"

Margaret simply stood there, a disbelieving look about her as she watched the old rancher march back to the main house. By the time he'd disappeared from view, Dennison had saddled himself a bronc from the corral and walked it over to where the Kid waited for him.

"Woodrow, please don't go. Please." Her plea went unanswered as the two boys mounted up. Dennison gave her a slow shake of his head, the kind that wasn't so much a no answer as it was one of disappointment. He was telling her that he wouldn't be coming back and she knew it. And the dam busted.

She cried into my chest for a minute or so as they rode

off, taking one last look when the pair were no more than a cloud of dust on the horizon.

"I love him, Dallas, I really do," she said desperately, looking up at me with those big brown eyes. "You know that, don't you? Please tell me you do."

I took her in my arms and hugged her like a little girl I once knew long ago and let her cry until there wasn't anything left in her. "Sure, darlin', I know," I spoke softly into her ear as the cloud of dust became no more than a speck of dust on the open range. "I was just sort of hoping that somehow he knew too."

CHAPTER FOURTEEN

Things were never the same after that, but then, I reckon the only thing that don't change is those mountains I trapped way back in my youth. After what had happened of late, I found myself thinking of them more and more. Maybe it was time to move on. Riding for the brand was the way of things out here, but I wasn't a rider and had always been more of a loner than anything else. So maybe it was time.

Besides, things had quieted down some since the Brady killing and that shoot-out at Blazer's Mill. Buckshot Roberts had died the day after the shooting, just like we all knew he would. You don't survive being gut shot out here. Hell, that may be the only time you do some real personal praying to your Maker and hope the agony will end quickly. A grand jury had been formed to look into the deaths of Brady and Roberts, and there was some question as to whether we did or didn't have a sheriff in Lincoln County. And to top it off, a couple of newspaper editors were soon ready to have a shoot-out of their very own over this Lincoln County issue. Yes, maybe it was time to move on.

It wasn't but an hour after sunup the day after Sonny had left that I heard the fall of the ax outside the cookshack and took a gander out the doorway. I could have guessed who it was. Or maybe I should've been getting used to it by now. Margaret Dawson was dressed in jeans and another man's shirt, her hair pulled back in a ponytail so as not to get in her way as she swung the ax.

"Working out the feisty in you?" I smiled.

"Well, someone's got to do it!" she said, stubbornly, sounding as though she could be as belligerent as some of the ranch hands.

"True," I admitted. "Moughts well be done by a young wildcat as any, I reckon."

"Flattery will get you nowhere." She took a hefty swing at one of the bigger chunks of deadwood, planting the blade a good ways into it for being as skinny as she was. Trouble was she couldn't get the blade worked back out and the piece was too heavy for her to lift.

"Never has, missy," I said, taking the ax handle and its heavy attachment in hand. She stood back as I wielded the piece back and up over my head, bringing it down in a resounding crash that split the deadwood in half as well as a few other chunks that flew about. "Usually just gets me in trouble." I shrugged, handed the ax back to her. "Most folks can't take honesty all that well, I reckon."

Half an hour later she was inside, reaching for the dipper, looking a wee bit peaked from swinging that ax. On the pretense of pouring myself some coffee, I got a glance at a fair-sized pile of wood she had taken care of.

"Does it always get this hot?"

I smiled. "Only when you work."

At first I wasn't sure if she was going to bite back or let it pass. When she gave me a mock frown, I knew I was safe. She got some more water, sipped at it slowly.

"How do you stand it? All of the heat, all of the dryness? It was hardly ever this way back East." She seemed genuinely interested for a woman who, the day before, was acting as though her heart had been broken. And I'll admit that the calmness with which she approached that ax and woodpile did have me curious. I couldn't recall seeing all that many women who'd gotten over what they called a broken heart as fast as this one.

"You're in a different land now, missy. We specialize in gila monsters and rattlesnakes, not river rats and bogged-down woodland. Why, shoot, girl, this ain't nothing! You shoulda been here a couple, three years ago ary you want to find out what hot is. Went so long without water that when a drop of water fell in one man's face we had to bring him to by throwing a couple buckets of dirt in his face!" She laughed at the exaggeration and it seemed like a good sign, so I stretched the blanket just a wee bit more while I finished my coffee. "Drought got really bad that summer, as I recall. Really bad. Wasn't nothing growing but dirt. Fact is, old Tom Lang come in one day and told Uncle John that ary those cattle on the back forty didn't get 'em something to eat pretty quick, why, we was gonna have beef jerky on the hoof!" I strung it out like any good storyteller, surprised looks and all, and had her laughing again.

"You're funny, Dallas." She said it just like a little girl does to her daddy when she's too young, too innocent to know how harsh the real world can be.

"Comes with the territory," I said, my smile disappearing. "Sometimes it helps—" I was going to say that sometimes it helps ease the hurt, but she knew that already and was in my arms, holding on to me for dear life, crying all over again, just like yesterday. "I reckon that's one part of the body that takes the longest to heal," I said softly.

"What's that?" she asked, looking up at me with eyes that were once again red from crying.

"The heart, darlin', the heart."

"Well, now, ain't that a pretty picture." The voice was that of Uncle John, but it came from behind me and like I say, I'm not all that fond of that.

"Damn it, John, I swear I'm gonna rig up that Greener of mine so's I can hang it by my side and just blow the hell outta the next person that walks up behind me like that."

"I'll keep that in mind, Dallas." He gave my kitchen a quick once-over, walked over to the coffeepot and hefted it to see how full it was. "You know, I was thinking, I might be able to get Margaret to ride in and get our mail, but what with things being the way they are . . . well, you wouldn't mind tagging along with her, would you?"

For being shorthanded I was caught up with what needed being done so far in the day, especially with that wood that Margaret had readied for me.

"Any of them mustangs in the corral lady-broke?" I asked.

"Oh, I think we can find one that's gentle enough for Miss Margaret."

It didn't take too long to get saddled up and ready to ride, and when we were Uncle John only had one other comment.

"Don't spend too much time with Kate, Dallas. Remember, you've still got a meal to fix for tonight."

That girl knew how to handle a horse. There might be some question as to handling a man, but not a horse. We rode like the wind to get to Lincoln and never once did Margaret Dawson have any trouble with her mount, which, by the way, wasn't quite as gentle as she may have been led to believe. We stopped to pick up the mail and then headed for the Montano store to see Kate.

"Well, now, isn't this a pleasant surprise," Kate said with that smile of hers. "Where's Sonny? I thought he'd be with you."

"Just come for the mail, Kate. As for Sonny, I reckon she can tell you," I said, glancing at Margaret.

The two of them talked for a while as I inspected the far side of the store, looking more for something to do than anything else. But I had to admit that I was wondering what would happen to the Dennison boy just as much as the women were. But there was no telling. He was an oddball, someone who simply hadn't fit in, not from the start. He could be easily persuaded in one direction or another and that wasn't always a good sign out here, for a man—or even a boy wanting to be a man—had to make up his own mind as to what was right and wrong. Life was like that in general but even more so out here because of the temptations that offered themselves up to a body. In Dennison's case it wasn't the red light district that had me worried as much as it was his association with Billy Bonney. The Kid was in bad enough company as it was and getting another youngster his age in with the same crowd wasn't going to add any years to anyone's life.

"Give me some .44-40's, .45's and shotgun shells, Kate," I said, after I figured the two women had gossiped enough. It surprised me in a way that Margaret had held up so well in telling Kate about Sonny and what had happened. Maybe I was overlooking something in her.

"Sounds like you're getting ready for a war." Kate's remark was casual as she dug underneath the counter and produced the required boxes of shells, but I thought I caught a hint of concern in her voice.

"Sort of a side war, if what I hear is right," I said, and told her about Lang spotting some rustlers on the Jinglebob. "Ain't enough that everyone in Lincoln County is trying to kill one another off, now we got some more scoundrels to deal with."

"You're the one who's a scoundrel, Dallas," she said, reaching across the counter and pulling my face far enough in to give it a kiss.

"Kate! You know better'n to—"

"I never thought I'd see the day," Margaret said in pure disbelief. "Why, a crusty old man like you . . . blushing." It might have surprised her, but it pleased her too and you can bet it made me nervous. See, told you I don't do well around women.

"Look, Kate, we gotta git. But do me a favor, will you?"

"Anything." She leaned on the counter, giving me one hellacious look of desire.

"Turk Calder or anyone with him come in that don't look familiar, see can you get their monicker for me. I got a hunch Tom Lang and John Chisum'll be right interested in where his sticks a-floating."

I'd cut my visit way short of what I would've liked it to be, so when we saddled up I told Margaret that there wasn't any need to rush for we had plenty of time to get back to the Chisum spread. Besides, riding horseback with a possibles sack full of live ammunition never did appeal to the horse racer in me—hell of a way for you and your mount to end your life. Hell of a way.

"Good," Margaret said, mounting up. "Perhaps you'll let me do the storytelling this time."

I shrugged. "Fair 'nough."

That she did, for by the time we were back to Chisum's, I knew a lot more about Woodrow Dennison than he'd ever felt like confiding in me. But he'd felt strongly enough about Margaret Dawson to spend that afternoon at the picnic telling her all about him while Kate and me were . . . talking.

He was sure enough from the East all right. Had a right smart education to boot. Could have gotten into one of those fancy universities but chose to accompany Margaret on her trip out here. Grew up with an aunt or grandmother who'd taken him in when his parents had died. He was eight years old by then and in a way that was bad because you tend to get used to your ma and pa by then. But being farmed out was nothing new, whether it was back East or out here, it was just the way of things. The woman who brought up Dennison must've been more overbearing than Turk Calder. She'd berated the boy enough to make him self-conscious of damn near everything he did, which explained some of his actions, both in and out of my kitchen. Never felt like he belonged, and I reckon that's important to a person no matter where they live. So he figured heading West would give him his manhood.

"And in the process he fell in love with me," she said sadly. "It sounded incredibly stupid when he said it that afternoon and I told him it was impossible. I even laughed at him." It didn't take a fool to see that she was as ashamed as a body can get over making that remark. It also explained the sour looks each had given the other on the way back that day. She went on to admit that she had been flirting with both Sonny and Tom Lang, playing one against the other for her feelings, something else I could see she wasn't too proud of.

"Then, when Tom Lang tried kissing me the day after . . ." The sentence trailed off as the young girl blushed, questioning herself as to whether she dare reveal her most private thoughts. "It was like it was happening right out of a storybook, the way he came to my rescue. I know it sounds strange, but when it was happening, when it was over, I knew he really loved me." The blush deepened but with it came an undeniable look of pride to her face. "I knew I loved him then too. Without a doubt."

"That was the impression I got," I said, remembering holding her in my arms like some poor child scared half out of her wits.

"Where will he go? What will become of him, Dallas?" A tone of desperation entered her voice now, telling me that she was genuinely concerned for the boy.

"Don't know, Margaret," I replied, calling her by her first name for the first time that I could remember. "But one thing he's gonna have to do is stop quitting and running out."

"I don't understand."

"If being a man is his prime ambition, he's gone about it in the wrong way," I said, cocking a frowning eye at her. We'd been exchanging truths so far this ride and this was no time to head down the wrong canyon, so truth is what she got. "He's either quit or run out on everything he's done so far. Didn't have the guts to stand up to them fancy pants back East, so he run away from 'em.

"Only time he felt comfortable that I can recall was

when the boys first got introduced to him and made him feel at home. Then, when he showed he was better at shooting off his mouth than he was a six-gun and got disapproval from the boys and me, why, he taken off. Done the same thing to you, too. Run out on you 'cause he didn't get his way.

"Well, that ain't the way it's done out here, missy." I'd worked up a good bit of anger and was letting her know what those fancy courtroom judges call "the truth, the whole truth and nothing but the truth." "Ary he loved you, that boy'd have stood his ground and fought Chisum, Lang and me if that's what it took. No one's gonna respect him until he can do that. No man in these parts that I know of, anyway.

"What'll happen to him? I don't know Margaret. But I'll tell you one thing. I don't think riding off with Billy the Kid as a companion was showing too much horse sense."

"What is it about this Billy the Kid, or whoever he is?" she asked. "They seem to treat him as if he's some kind of legend out here."

"Bad man to tangle with, that's what I told Sonny. You seen that yesterday. Some say he's good, some say he's bad. Likely a mixture of both. That still don't make it too healthful for Sonny to be riding with him."

"Why do you say that?" she said, her face looking more concerned than curious or confused.

"Something I've observed for a long time in this land, darlin'." Once again it was the truth she'd be getting. I just took my time saying it. "No man who ever became a legend in his own time ever lived too awful long. I don't know 'bout you, Margaret, but as stupid as some of the things Sonny's pulled are, I'd hate to see him get caught in the cross fire when Billy Bonney's time comes."

That was the end of that conversation as she put her

heels to her mount and raced ahead of me back to the ranch.

And the Chisum crew had their supper on time that night.

CHAPTER FIFTEEN

You'd think that with all of that work we did from can see to can't see out here, there wouldn't be time left for much of anything else and a lot of times there wasn't. But one thing you learn out here right quick if you want to stay with an outfit is that you'd better have a sense of humor. Why, son, it'd drive you mad in no time if you didn't! Guaranteed. I reckon that's why some of us who figure we don't have much time left after the day's work is done sort of fit our humor in with the chores.

"DALLAS!!!" The voice was loud and shrill, and I'd gotten used enough to the differences between the two women on the Chisum spread to know that it belonged to Uncle John's niece, Sallie. I stopped the unloading I was doing and casually took a gander at Sallie Chisum, standing on that veranda as red as a beet and ready to bust a vein any second now. I don't know if you've ever run across that look on a woman they describe as a woman scorned, but Sallie had it now and that seemed right dangerous, considering that she didn't have herself a beau to be scorned over.

"What could she want in such a hurry?" Margaret asked, sticking her flour-covered head out of the cookshack. It had been two weeks now since Sonny had left with the Kid, and the girl had been helping me out where she could, graduating from wood chopping to biscuit and pie making. At the moment Miss Margaret was working on some fancies for the boys.

"Beats me," I said. "You just git back to work, young lady.

I'll take care of this." I'll say this, she was catching on a lot quicker than the Dennison boy had. Why, she was getting so good at what I taught her . . . But that's a whole 'nother canyon.

"Hold on now, Sallie," Chisum said, a bit more stand-offish than he might otherwise be. Hell, I'd be that way too around a woman who could yell like that! "Let's not start pulling out the Winchesters until we know we've got a fight on our hands."

"How could you!!" the woman yelled out. Actually, she wasn't any younger or older than Margaret Dawson, but this didn't seem like the time to be discussing the differences between being a girl and a woman.

I'd been in to Lincoln to get supplies that morning and had picked up the mail and dropped it off at the main house upon returning. I hadn't given it a thought until I saw the letter and envelope Sallie Chisum was waving angrily at me. It was then something in the back of my mind told me I'd better be cautious, *real cautious.* I couldn't pin it down exactly, and by the time I'd approached the veranda and the furious woman standing on it . . . well, it was too late.

"Well, don't just stand there, Uncle John, DO SOME-THING!" she commanded, still red as can be.

"Now, you just hold it right there, Sallie." Now, that was the John Chisum I knew. Man wouldn't take nothing from nobody. He turned to the woman, who now looked like a girl, planted both hands on his hips and spoke in an even sterner voice, if that was possible. "It'll be a cold day in hell before *you* start giving *me* orders around here. Now, you just simmer down until we find out what's going on," he said, firmly in control of the situation now. Anyone else would've grabbed the letter out of Sallie's hand, but in the case of John Chisum . . . well, let's just say he's spent more time on the range than he ever has in a schoolhouse so he couldn't have read it anyway.

"Boss, unless you got something urgent, I got a whole lot

of unloading to do," I said, yanking a thumb over my shoulder at the half-empty wagon. Now, you may think that was some kind of excuse but it wasn't. Well, almost.

"It seems that Sallie here has run into a difficulty of sorts, Dallas," John said, giving me one of his official looks. "Matter of fact, she says you're the cause of it."

"And how do you figure that?" I said, although I was certain I already knew what it concerned. Still, I pretended to listen while Uncle John spun the story.

Everyone knows that no self-respecting cowhand ever catered to drinking milk once he got past being weaned as a youngster. Milk to a cattleman was like comparing six-shooter coffee to that back East tea they drink in those dainty little cups. It was about as worthless as putting buffalo chips in one of those green salads I saw made one time. Besides, it came from cows and the cattleman associated cows with farmers, another species he had no great love for. But that didn't stop milk from being made.

What John was telling me now, and what I suspected this ruckus was about, was how the Carnation Company, who fancied themselves right smart for producing what they called condensed milk, had set out earlier in the year to find a verse that any woman entering the contest thought good enough to be put on their cans of milk. Some sort of prize was being offered, although I never paid much mind to what it was.

"You just ask him, Uncle John," Sallie said, pointing an accusing finger at me when her uncle had finished speaking. "I gave him the address to that Carnation Company and told him to mail the letter on the way into town a few months back. Now, I get this back!" She was about ready to bust into tears.

"Why, sure I taken that letter in and mailed it," I said, giving my jeans a hitch.

"Mailed it as it was?"

"You bet." I pushed my hat back, trying to look innocent as all hell. "Why? What's the fuss?"

"This letter, here," John said, holding it up in his hand, "says that what they got was the most obscene thing they'd ever received." He paused a moment, cocked an almost frowning eye at me. "She thinks you tampered with her letter, Dallas. That's what the fuss is."

"Now, John, you know me better'n that." He did, which is likely why he got in a real hurry.

"He says he didn't, Sallie." But she didn't look like she was buying any of it today. "Look, you write the company a letter for me and I'll tell 'em they got the wrong letter, got it mixed up with another. It's just a big mistake, you'll see." I don't think I've ever seen Sallie scowl as deep as she did then, a look of defeat on her face as she stomped back inside.

I was halfway across the yard, heading toward my supply wagon, when I heard John's voice again.

"Unloading it all by yourself."

"Yup." I unloaded a couple of cases in silence before I noticed that Uncle John wasn't doing much more than standing there, watching me. "Just come over to see can I do my job, did you?" You may have noticed that I don't take kindly to being the only one working when there's plenty of it around to be done and I'm the only one doing it.

"I want to know, Dallas." I gave him an I-don't-know-what-you're-talking-about look, even though both of us knew what he was talking about. "What was it you put in that letter of Sallie's that got those folks so riled up?" Conversational was how he said it, not high and mighty like some will. John Chisum knows how I feel about that. Just the same, he was going to find out what was going on.

So I told him.

"It just didn't have no punch to it, John. None a-tall."

Carnation milk in the little red can
The very best there is in the land.

That was what Miss Sallie had originally written, and it was as bland as the contents of the can it would go on to my mind.

"And you decided to . . . punch it up some, did you?"

"Well—" Hesitant wasn't the word to describe how slowly I spoke now. John and I had come a long ways together, and I would have hated to have a misunderstanding be the end of it.

"I wonder, Dallas," he said now, rubbing a hand across the stubble that was beginning to form on his chin, "you think you might remember just how much you punched those lines up?"

"Oh, considerable, John, considerable."

"What'd it sound like?"

"You sure you want to hear?" He nodded. "Well, John, that poem had real flavor to it when them Easterners got it, yes, it did." Then I took a step back as I recited the poem as Carnation had received it.

"Carnation milk in the little red can
Very best there is in the land
No tit to squeeze, no hay to pitch
Just punch a hole in the sonofabitch."

He tried to keep a serious look about him, but wound up laughing just the same. When he stopped laughing, he gave me a look that said I shouldn't have done it, but he understood why. You get to know a body after a while. He didn't say much else until he was walking away. Then he stopped and gave me one of those mischievous smiles.

"You know, Dallas, if I was you I'd keep an eye on those cleavers of yours."

"Cleavers?" I didn't understand.

"Yes. You see, Dallas, when the day comes you find one of

'em missing, I've got a strong notion you'll find out how old Santos felt."

"Santos?"

"Yes." The smile widened, the way it will when some-one's about to tell you something you don't know but know you should. "When you find one of 'em missing, you can bet it'll be Sallie who's gotten hold of it. You see, Dallas, that'll be the day I tell her what *really* happened to her letter."

With that he left, still grinning from ear to ear. Like I said, out here you've got to have a sense of humor.

Trouble was, I didn't know if Uncle John was funning me or not!

Now, friend, I don't get shaken easily, and that letter Miss Sallie had sent in, well, that was just a harmless prank. After she cooled down, I knew that Sallie Chisum would forget about the whole thing and not give it a second thought—I think. What did shake my confidence for a while was Miss Margaret.

One of the reasons I'd taken her on was the knowledge that Kate had told her the recipe for that fried chicken. And you'd better believe that I was going to do everything in my power to get that recipe out of my new assistant. After all, a cook's got his pride. And I can string a greener as well as anyone in this world. It was when Miss Margaret stuck that flour-covered face out the side door where I'd been unloading my supplies as Uncle John left that I had my doubts. Aside from the flour and sweat, her face had that impish look some youngsters get when they've gotten away with something and know it and want you to know it as well. I don't know about you, but to me it's as unsettling as hell.

"Dallas," she smiled, "you may *never* get Kate's recipe for fried chicken now."

She'd heard us! Heard it all! Me and John talking right

outside the cookshack about that letter of Sallie's and she'd heard it all!

Now, ain't that just like a woman? If they can't get you one way, they'll get you another!

CHAPTER SIXTEEN

"We got trouble," Tom Lang said, reining his mount to a halt in front of my cookshack. It wasn't me he was talking to though. Hell, nobody comes to a cook unless he's *really* got troubles he wants to spill his guts about. No, Lang was spouting off to Uncle John, who'd come out to see how Margaret Dawson was doing. Fact is, he'd done it often enough to where I was wondering if I wasn't treating her like some slave. Which, of course, I wasn't. Well, almost.

"If it's Turk Calder again, I thought you said we already had trouble with him and his merry little band," Chisum said, his tone of voice changing from pleasant to disturbed in a matter of seconds. But maybe I shouldn't have been surprised at it, for it was getting to be a normal change of mood these days in Lincoln County, at least from what I'd observed.

"We do," the foreman said, dismounting and catching his breath as I handed him a dipper of water. "But it ain't just Calder, if what I heard him say was right."

"Spoke to him, did you? Face to face?" I must've had the same look of disbelief on my face as Uncle John did at that last bit Tom Lang had offered.

"Yeah." It was that satisfied sort of smile I'd seen on his face and that of every other cowhand after finishing a meal, the kind that tells anyone noticing it that he deserved that good a meal after that hard a day's work. "Face to face. Me and a couple of the boys set up a little ambush this morning, and just like I figured, Turk Calder and his crew walked into it."

"That so." A mite of worry came to Uncle John's face now and I knew he was wondering how many men and cattle he'd lost because of Lang's actions. I reckon the foreman knew that look too.

"Me, Charlie and Shorty caught 'em working the south end of the herd, Mr. Chisum," he said by way of explanation. "At least they *thought* they'd be working that part of the herd. Turk ain't too good at explanations," he smiled.

"No man is when he's looking down the business end of another man's weapon," I said. Feel sort of left out if I don't throw in some of that sage advice every once in a while.

"They ain't brush poppers, Mr. Chisum, I can guarantee you that. Only brush Turk Calder or his boys ever run smack into was when they was clearing a trail because John Law was following it. *Pistoleros,* border ruffians maybe, but the closest they ever come to working beef was with a knife and a fork."

"It figures," Uncle John said, knowing that all you had to do was start something like this Lincoln County fandango to keep your attention while small-time rustlers ate away at your herd, bit by bit. "But wasn't that just a bit foolish, Lang?" he asked as the mad started coming out in him, realizing what could have happened. "If Calder had those six men you say he did before and there was only three of you—"

Talk about war! For a second there I thought Tom Lang was about to wage it on Chisum himself! Oh, the mad showed up in his face all right, but not as much as the frustration I saw in him as he spoke.

"You know, Mr. Chisum, I expect to get a hard time from cookie, here, and the boys. I expect it from that Dennison kid and Bonney and Calder just because of who they are, but it would sure be a change if I didn't get it from you too." He had his hands planted firmly on his hips and could've been talking to a younger brother he could no longer tolerate, what with the screwed-up look and that badgering voice he had.

"Well, those cattle could've—"

"Those cattle could've stampeded if shots had been fired but they weren't, Chisum. And as for those gunmen, well, let me tell you people something." That was fire in his eyes, friend, and you'd better believe it was telling you to sit up and take notice, which is just what we did. "I was sixteen when I joined Ben McCulloch back when the war broke out. He never expected nothing less of his men than he had of them when he was a Ranger. 'Ride like a Comanche, shoot like a Tennessean and fight like the very devil himself,' that's what they claimed the qualifications were, and before that war was over I could've been a Ranger. Oh, I may not be as fast as that Bonney character, but don't you ever doubt that I could've shot those birds right outta their saddles and never got a scratch." He tossed me the empty dipper and prepared to mount up.

"Now, wait a minute," Uncle John said, "you said there was trouble. Just what're you talking about?"

He was ready to fork the saddle but stopped, his cold, hard glare returning to Big John Chisum.

"I told Calder that if I ever caught the sonofabitch on Jinglebob range again, I'd kill him. Pardon, ma'am," he said, noticing Margaret standing in the doorway. I reckon she'd been there the whole while, although this was the first time I'd taken note of her.

"Oh, that's all right," she said, "I've picked up a whole new vocabulary working here with Dallas."

"That so," Uncle John said, raising a concerned eyebrow at me. And if you don't think that was unsettling . . . well, you see what I mean about women? But there wasn't enough time for a discussion about that.

"Calder said there's a faction down in Seven Rivers that's ready to take sides in this Lincoln County issue. Says when they get up here he'll bring them and the Evans gang *and*

take us all on." He didn't have to emphasize the last of
what he said to make John or me know what he meant by
trouble.

Like I say, Jesse Evans and his crowd were doing the
same thing for Dolan and Murphy that Dick Brewer and
Billy the Kid had supposedly been doing for Alexander
McSween and John Chisum. Hearing about those from
Seven Rivers didn't make any one of us feel any the more
easy about it.

"I don't understand," Margaret said. "What's so bad
about this Seven Rivers place?"

"They say there ain't no law or God west of the Pecos,
ma'am," Lang said.

"That's right," I added. "And don't you believe it's just
the west part of Texas. Mind you, I ain't never been there,
missy, but from what I hear of Seven Rivers, why, I'd say
the only thing the town's got going for itself is breeding
meanness to those that're already mean."

"It also sounds like a place Turk Calder might've picked
up those *pistoleros* you're talking of," Uncle John said to his
foreman.

"Bet on it," was the big man's only reply. But whatever
the two of them were thinking, I was way ahead of them.

"Say, boss, I was thinking. Mebbe this mought not be a
bad time to stock up on some more supplies. Lay in for the
winter, ary you know what I mean," I said, except it wasn't
what I was saying at all and Uncle John knew it. I was
looking for an excuse to get in to see Kate again and maybe
get her the hell out of Lincoln.

"Well," John drawled, "I reckon we could stand a few
more supplies, Dallas. You won't be too long, will you?"

"I'll go along," Tom Lang said, adding, "to help cookie
load up those supplies," when Chisum began to take him in
suspiciously. Other than that he didn't comment on the
statement, but I had a notion Uncle John knew there was
more than that involved.

"You wasn't really serious 'bout riding with McCulloch back there, were you?" I asked Lang as he helped me with the riggings to the team and wagon.

"Dead serious, cookie." He'd stopped what he was doing, as though to lend full concentration to me and what was said next. "Like you say, Dallas, never call a man a liar just because he knows more than you do."

"Right," I replied, and went back to rigging up the team, making a mental note never to question Tom Lang on Ben McCulloch, the Texas Rangers or his abilities with a pistol or rifle.

"And where do you think you're going?" I asked as I pulled the wagon around front only to see Margaret Dawson brushing her hands off as she donned her hat.

"With you, of course." She said it pleasant enough but I knew where we were heading was no place for a lady, young or otherwise.

"Not hardly!" I growled from my seat.

"But—"

"Who the hell do you think is gonna get the fixin's ready while I'm gone, young lady?" When she said nothing, I punctuated the air with that stubby old finger of mine she'd yet to get used to. *"You,* that's who. Now, git to it!"

"But who's going to cut up the wood?" she asked helplessly. "Who'll cut the beef?"

"Get him to do it," Lang said from atop his mount. "He can tell you what it's like to work for that sonofabitch, Chisum." Smiled when he said that, you bet.

"Me!?" Uncle John was downright surprised.

"Why, sure, John, you remember, don't you?" I said, maybe pushing it some but enjoying it all the same. "It's just like the good old days . . . called earning your keep, as I recall it."

With that I got the team moving, but not before I heard Uncle John call out my name. Due for another cussing about who it was that run this outfit, I figured. But it wasn't that, not that at all.

"You tell Kate I got room for her out here any time she wants." Then he spit on one hand, rubbed both together and picked up the ax. "Come on, girl," he said to Margaret, "we got us a ranch to run."

Like I said, John Chisum knows me pretty well.

Turk Calder was a drinker, no matter what time of the day or night. And if he'd been spited by a woman or backed down by a man, you can bet he took to a bottle with the full intention of getting as ugly and mean drunk as could be. It wasn't until halfway to Lincoln that it crossed my mind that that was the reason Tom Lang was coming to town with me. Getting and loading supplies was as much an excuse for him as it was for me. I was wanting to check up on Kate, and he was doing the same thing on Turk Calder—and maybe more.

The rest of the time riding into town I had Kate Rogers on my mind. Trouble was I wasn't sure I could do much more than protect her, and a woman like Kate deserved more than that. I knew what it was she had in mind, trapping me into marriage like all women do to a man. But what could I give her? I had no money, although I sure did hold a lot of it for the boys at one time or another. No real place to call a home, not even if you counted my cookshack. Oh, I was convincing myself more and more each day that I was maybe in love with her, but that held about as much hope as the dreams those fools had on their way to the California gold fields back in '49. No, it was time to move on, time to let Kate get on with her life as soon as I knew she'd be safe. Yup, that's what I'd do, I'd talk it all out with her when we got the supplies. Get it over with once and for all.

"You can stop mumbling to yourself, Dallas," Lang said, bringing me back to the here and now, "we're here now."

He had a gleam in his eye but it wasn't from looking at my ugly face. No, sir. Riding down the main street, he'd spotted some horses tied up in front of the saloon, and I'd bet a year's pay it was knowing they belonged to Calder and his crowd that brought the gleam to his eye. Yes, Turk Calder was what Lang had come for.

"Tom," I said, getting his attention as I turned the rig down the back alley to the side of the Montano store.

"Yeah."

"Afore you start dancing, we load my supplies, understood?" There was no way in hell I was going to load or unload any supplies if I had to go through the same experience I had nearly a month ago here.

"Sure, Dallas." He had that devil-may-care look, like the boy who's found the cookie jar and is about to partake of the goodies inside. But something in the back of my mind told me Tom Lang was going to get caught, but good.

Kate was as rosy-cheeked and bright as ever when we entered the store. Surprised too, for being as quiet as she was.

"Come for supplies, Kate." Always get the business out of the way first when you're dealing with a woman. "Need every bit of .44-40 ammo you've got, as well as my shotgun shells. And throw in a couple extra Winchesters."

"Going to war, Dallas?" That must've been her cue, the reason why she was so quiet when we first walked in, for Billy the Kid and Sonny appeared from the back room.

"Can't be too careful, cookie," the Kid said. But what caught my eye was the Dennison boy.

"Well, now, would you lookee here." If I sounded amazed, well, I was. Sonny was a whole new person than from the last time I'd seen him. I figured it would be a while before the new rubbed off of him, but there was something different about the youngster standing before me now. He was wearing a John B., blue work shirt and jeans and likely, although I couldn't see them from where I stood, a pair of cowhide boots. His face wasn't as pale as it had been and bigger than God made green apples he was packing a brand-new Colt in just as new a holster, but that wasn't what had changed. What he'd done was fill out some from the skin and bones frame he'd arrived with. "Changed some, I see."

"You haven't." The smile caught me off guard for I was certain he'd still be mad about the way he'd left Chisum's. But he was being hospitable and you don't turn that down out here, not with the way things had been going of late. "How's Margaret?" he asked after a few moments of awkward silence.

"She misses you, Sonny," Tom Lang said before I could open my mouth. "A lot." And he meant it too! Maybe I was wrong, maybe this was why Lang had come to town with me.

"Tom, why don't I show you where I've got some of that ammunition Dallas is wanting," Kate said, and the two disappeared. And damn, did I feel awkward.

"Teach him how to use that thing?" I asked the Kid, giving Sonny's Colt a second look.

"He's getting passable."

Sonny blushed some. "Learned how to undo the thong first."

"Then he's got all the chance he needs." The voice came from my side, from the front door, and when I turned there was big, ugly Turk Calder, with a handful of his new henchmen behind him.

"You know, Turk, I'm getting awful tired of you." The Kid stepped out beside me, as ready to do the man in as I was.

"No, Billy, it's me he's wanting," Sonny said, walking forward with what appeared to be bravado. "We never did see eye to eye, did we, Turk?" Apparently, he was going to take him on then and there.

"Dallas, what's going on?" I heard Kate say from behind

me as she reentered the room, then a gasp and "Oh, my God!" as I turned to her, my Greener still resting on my hip, pointing toward Calder. She had the most fearful look I'd ever seen on her, a fist covering her mouth, a look of horror in her eyes as she stared at the crowd in her front doorway.

"Back out, Calder," I said. When none of them moved, I yelled, "NOW!" and they got the hint. Or maybe they moved out of the doorway because the Kid and Sonny simply walked past me, guns drawn, looking like they meant business.

"It's him, Dallas," Kate said, still standing where she originally entered. "My God, it's him!"

"Who? What are you talking about, Kate?"

"The fire . . . Dan . . . the killing," she said, nowhere near the Montano store from the look of her eyes. No, she was reliving that horror she'd told me about, seeing it all again. "Don't you see, he's the one who got away!" Protect her was all I could think to do and somehow I would, somehow I'd protect my Kate.

"It'll be all right, darlin'," I said, taking her in my arms and noticing how comfortable she felt inside them. "Don't you worry none. You just tell me which one he is."

"There," she said, looking past me, "the one with the medium build with the rope burn around his neck. The one with the long black hair."

I winked at her, smiled. "You get that smile back on your face, woman. I don't like them scary looks."

By the time I'd gotten outside, Greener in hand, I could've killed the whole lot of them just for being who they were. Fact is, from the look on the Kid and Sonny's faces, I'd have gotten all the assistance I wanted in doing it, too. And they knew it, brother, they knew it!

"I'm betting you're just as inexperienced with your fists as you are with that six-shooter, Sonny," Calder said in that mean-as-hell voice he had. That was Turk's real calling, I reckon, being able to draw you into a fight and do it on his grounds, which was just what he was doing with Sonny.

"And I've taken your flannel-mouthed talk for the last time," was Sonny's reply as he holstered his pistol. Normally, if you want to impress someone out here you hit them betwixt the eyes with a water-logged piece of deadwood, but I had to admit that what I'd seen in the last few minutes made me think the boy might have a chance in this land after all. But then, Mama always said the proof was in the pudding, and we hadn't even set down to the table yet.

"Sorry, kid," Billy said, holstering his own Colt, "can't help you on this one." With a weak smile, he added, "Guns are my specialty, not fists."

There are some times in life when you just have to speak your mind, no matter what the consequences may be. I knew I had a good chance of being gunned down by the Kid when I said it, but to me it was worth it. "Some goddamn *compadre* you are," I growled at him. I was about to turn to the Dennison boy and tell him what a fool he was for getting in with the likes of Billy the Kid, when three of the plug uglies on the Kid's side of me began to draw their pistols. I reckon that was what Turk had in mind, getting us to put away our guns and keep our attention on him while these three yahoos did us in. Like I say, the business end of a Colt is mighty scary.

Except they didn't shoot.

Oh, they drew all right, and may even have had those guns cocked, but another gun from my left rear went off and those *pistoleros* got unarmed right quick. I looked at the Kid but his gun was still in his holster!

"Now do you believe me, Dallas?"

"Jesus Christ and J. B. Hickok," I said slowly. Mind you, now, I don't get awestruck much these days, but the only other person I'd ever seen do shooting that fancy was James Butler Hickok himself, and he'd been dead for two years now! Yet, there was Tom Lang, smoking gun in hand, standing there with that silly grin he'd had when we came to town. And you know something, hoss, if he'd have told me he was a cousin of Hickok's . . . why, I do believe I wouldn't have questioned it at all because he could damn sure shoot like him!

"That's something else you want to keep in mind about surviving in this land, Sonny," he said, although his gaze was on Turk Calder. "Never say you're gonna do something for the last time." He must've heard Sonny's exchange with Calder from that back room where the supplies were. "I hadn't been here just now, that would have been the last time you'd ever have taken any talk from old flannel mouth, there. You do have a point though, son. Turk Calder's always had more lip than a muley cow."

You don't describe the rage Calder was feeling at that moment. You just sort of watch to see if he'll pop a vein and die right where he stands, or charge like the mad bull he was.

"Kid, why don't you take these three birds to the town limits, put their guns in their saddlebags and wish 'em a fond farewell."

"You can't run us out of town!" one of them objected in what was so far the only show of force put up by any of them other than drawing those guns.

"Maybe I'm not *supposed* to, mister, but don't even suggest that I can't, because I am. My advice to you is to head back to Seven Rivers, or further south if you've a mind to, but if I see you three on Jinglebob range, or in this town for that matter, well, fellas, I'm gonna kill you."

And that was that as far as Tom Lang was concerned. Watching him calmly put three more beans in the wheel of his own pistol, I had a feeling he'd done more than ranch hand work in his lifetime. A lot more.

That left Rope Burn, the fellow Kate had so terrifyingly described in the store, and Turk Calder. Rope Burn, he was beginning to squint at Kate, who now stood beside me out in the street, trying to identify her from some other place he'd seen her. A flash of recognition came to his eyes, followed by a slow grin that began forming on his face. Seeing that grin was enough to make me hate his guts forever, however long that was going to be.

"I can still take you," Calder said, focusing his attention on Sonny once again. "I don't need a gun or gunmen." He was balling up his fists, looking for a fight now more than ever.

"Didn't seem like that a minute ago," Sonny said, acting just as calmly as the Kid would. He'd not only filled out his physical build but his mind too, in a manner of speaking. "As I recall, your three friends were about to cut us to ribbons."

"You're gonna pay for that!" Calder took an angry step toward Sonny, but I stepped in between the two.

"Now, wait a minute," I said. "I can see I'm gonna have to explain the rules to you two. Here, darlin', hold this," I added, tossing my Greener to Kate, who looked as baffled as the two antagonists I stood between.

"Rules? What rules?" Calder asked.

"Why, the rules of Marcus, that English fella that invented all of this fair play fighting. Besides, range cooks always explain the finer points of fights like this. It's range law." I knew that Sonny was too green to understand what I was talking about, and Turk Calder, well, he might be big and strong, but his brain was addled about as much as my aunt Martha's when it came to knowing what a range cook did and didn't do. So you see, you can't ever say that us biscuit shooters lack in imagination. Besides, with what I had in mind, I was about to do my protecting of Kate Rogers.

"Now, you two pay attention while I use this man here to show you just what I mean. Step forward, friend." Rope Burn was about as perplexed as the rest but he fell right into my trap and stepped forward. He was standing almost next to Turk now, at a ninety degree angle from my own stance. "To be a fair fight there's lots of things you don't do. For example, there'll be no throat punching," I said as the flat side of my left hand flew out and connected with Rope Burn's Adam's apple. I reckon everyone else was as surprised as he was, his mouth flapping open as a choking sound tried to come from it. "And no flat handing." I did a half left, bringing the flat of my right hand up against the man's jaw, slamming it shut. I noticed Turk smiling at what was going on as I stepped closer to Rope Burn and thrust an elbow in his brisket, knocking the wind out of him. "No elbowing." It was then that Sonny finally caught on to the time I was buying him and hit Turk twice real hard. That boy must've filled out some, for Calder fell backward, if only momentarily. The boy was on his own now, for I had my own fight—if that's what you want to call it—to take care of. A quick hand grabbed the dazed man behind the neck and brought his face down as I brought my knee up into it. "And no kneeing." There was blood on my pants leg when I pulled his head away from it and effortlessly tossed him backward and over.

I had no doubt that Tom Lang would kill Calder the moment things got too rough for Sonny, so I tended to the semiconscious man I'd just done in. He was likely only seeing a blur from where I stood so I squatted down beside him, placing one knee on his chest as I grabbed a chunk of his long black hair. The expression on his face told me he was conscious enough to feel the pain as I yanked at his scalp, so I knew he'd hear me and wouldn't forget.

"I don't know who the hell you are, mister," I said, for the first time aware that I was talking in a snarl, I was feeling that much hate, "and I don't much care. But if you never listen to anything else in your lifetime, make sure you hear what I'm saying now." I yanked harder at the fistful of hair, his eyes bulging with pain. *"Comprende?"*

He nodded, eager to please.

"You stay away from Kate Rogers, pilgrim, or I'll kill you on sight. She tells me she seen so much as a shadow of you around her and I'm gonna track you down. And don't you think that crowd down at Seven Rivers is gonna protect you. If it takes it, I'll kill half of them to get to you. I'd take a liking to them Canadian Rockies, was I you, and hivernate until I die of old age, which'll be some time from now." There was no question in his mind now that I meant what I said or would do any or all of it, that much I could see in his eyes.

"I didn't know there was anyone as ugly as Turk Calder." Tom Lang was standing there, a satisfied smile on his face. "I'd take his advice, mister," the big man said, looking past me as I got up. "Only a fool argues with a mule or a cook, and this one's a bit of both."

A loud thud behind me reminded me that Sonny and Turk were still going at it—I thought. When I turned I saw Turk kick the boy in the chest as he started to get up, sending him back down to the ground. I gave Lang a quick, hard glance, wanting to know how things were.

"He was holding his own just a minute ago," the foreman said. Then, pulling his gun, he said, "Looks like he's gonna need some help."

"You let him be. He can take care of himself," Billy the Kid said from his horse. He had quickly dispatched the gunmen and returned to what was still a good fight, if there is such a thing.

Turk was sitting on the boy now, Sonny doing all he could to block the blows from his assailant, blood dribbling down his cheek and the side of his mouth. Still, he seemed determined. Suddenly, he pushed his arms down beside him, pushing his midsection up, an effort which took some doing, as heavy as Turk was. There wasn't enough force the first time and he took a hard blow to the side of his head, but the second time he succeeded in rocking his huge opponent backward enough so those gangly legs of his could reach up and grasp Turk's head between them like a vise, pulling the upper portion of Turk's body down on his legs. In the same motion his right forearm came down hard on Turk's crotch and the big man let out a howl that could be heard all over town. Sonny pushed the man off of him, gained some balance on his knees and drove that bony fist of his into the small of Turk Calder's back. The cry of pain intensified as the man lay whimpering like a baby in the fetal position.

Turk Calder had been had, and Sonny was the one who'd done it. And all of Lincoln was there to see it, even if they were mostly hiding behind windows and doors.

"*That's* the kind of *compadre* I am, cookie," the Kid said, leaning forward in his saddle. "Taught him that my own self, I did."

"You said to finish what you start, didn't you?" Sonny asked, alternately shaking and rubbing his fists. Yes, there had definitely been a change in Woodrow Dennison since I'd last seen him.

"Señor," a young Mexican boy yelled out, skidding to a stop at the Kid's horse. "They come! I see the dust from the edge of town! The posse is come back!"

"You're a good scout, Paco," the Kid said, reaching in his pocket and flipping a two-bit piece into the air for the boy. "Better get your horse, Sonny, we gotta light a shuck."

"Sure, Billy." Sonny took a step, stopped, glanced back over his shoulder. "Tell Margaret I love her."

"Not a chance, son." When he gave me that quizzical look that said he didn't understand, I said, "That's something she'll find more believable ary it comes from you."

I reckon he understood but didn't have the time to comment on it, instead making his way to the alleyway where the Kid held his mount. He favored his side and didn't move as fast as he once might have, so maybe he was learning something about surviving out here after all.

Tom Lang seemed to have a new appreciation for the Kid, as much, it seemed, as I had for Sonny. For a man who once looked like he could have killed him on the spot, the big foreman had no disapproval of the Kid or his feistiness at all as we watched them leave.

"I'll get the wagon and my mount," he said as if nothing had happened. "We've got most all of what we came for in the way of ammunition, Dallas."

As he walked off, a handful of townsfolk came out and helped Turk Calder and Rope Burn—or whoever he was— off the streets. I took my Greener from Kate, who'd been silent the whole time, and headed back into the store to pick up those Winchesters I'd mentioned.

"You called me 'darling,'" she said as I got the rifles. "Twice."

"Oh. Well . . . just a slip of the tongue. I'll make sure it don't happen again." I could feel that red creeping up my back again.

"Oh, Dallas, you are a scoundrel." I don't know if you've ever been kissed by a woman with about three Winchesters cradled in your arms, but it's definitely an experience. Or maybe it was just the fact that it was Kate Rogers who was kissing me. And if I hadn't known we were going to need those rifles so badly, I'll tell you right now that I'd have gladly let go of them to take hold of her.

"I want you to leave the store, Kate, leave Lincoln," I said, knowing I'd better get it out of me now while I still had the guts to say it. "This place is gonna blow up one of these days and I don't want you anywhere nearby when it does. John says he'll make room for you at the main house." She was about to turn away, but I set the rifles down and took her by the arms, forcing her to face me. "Kate, you come out to the Jinglebob with me and you'll never have to wait to hear me say what Margaret Dawson's waiting for Sonny to say. Kate, I love you. I ain't had nothing and likely never will but—"

I never did get to finish what I was saying for she was kissing me again and you'd better believe that I kissed her right back. All I could think about was that Sunday picnic a few weeks back and how at ease she'd made me feel then, just like now. Yet, when we parted I knew at once that she wouldn't go.

"I can't, Dallas," she said in a low voice that was a mixture of pride and remorse. "I didn't run when they came after Dan and me, and I won't do it now. Don't you see, honey? It's the same thing you'd do, the same thing . . . Dan would have done."

"But he's gone, Kate," I said, likely sounding like a desperate man, and maybe I was. "I ain't Dan, I could never—"

"Yes, you are, Dallas," she said, placing a silent finger on my lips. "More than you'll ever know you're quite a bit like Dan was. You're kind and gentle and you know how to treat a lady, and I love you so very much. But I won't leave just to keep from getting hurt, just because I'm a woman."

There was a silence between us for a while then and I used it studying her every feature. But it still didn't get her any closer to the safety of the Chisum ranch.

"I won't say I understand your hardheadedness, woman, but you're right about what I'd do ary it was me in your position. Hell!" I finally said, then gave her a quick kiss, picked up the rifles and looked down at her. "You watch your topknot, woman, you hear?"

"Yes, darling." She was smiling when she said it, and happy about it to boot. And you know something, hoss, it didn't even make me blush when she said it.

It crossed my mind for the first time then that maybe that's how it's supposed to feel when two people are in love.

CHAPTER SEVENTEEN

You might say things sort of quieted down for a while after that, at least as far as gun play was concerned. Turk Calder and that friend of his that Kate thoroughly hated disappeared for a while, although I always had the feeling they weren't far off whenever someone would mention that Seven Rivers Gang that had appeared in the Lincoln area. Even saw the newly appointed sheriff jawing with Calder once while I was getting supplies at the Montano store. Should've been running him out of town like Tom Lang had those three others, but then, everyone knew that the sheriff was as much a Dolan man as any in the Seven Rivers crowd.

In June Uncle John went to St. Louis after injuring his leg while working with a horse. That left his brother, Jim, who was also Sallie's father, to look after the ranch.

I didn't see the Kid at all during that time, and if Sonny showed up to see Margaret Dawson it wasn't when I was around. But I could sense by the moods the girl got into once in a while that her longing for Sonny was still there and that she thought he wasn't coming back. She was filling out too, I reckon. Not in the physical sense, like Sonny had, but as my assistant cook. Even when she was feeling moody she knew there was a job to be done and did it without question or complaint. I'd taught her how to make deep dish apple pie, which the boys wanted seconds on, and all of the other fixings I'd planned on teaching Sonny if he'd stayed on long enough. But I still hadn't gotten that fried chicken recipe out of her that Kate said she knew. After a month or so I stopped trying, maybe because I was missing Sonny as much as she was. I just never said nothing about it. It'd be womanish to do so, for it wasn't like a man to show his emotions. Besides, another man's life—not to mention the problems that tend to go along with it—never made a soft pillow to sleep on. Me, I wasn't the kind to sit up all night long and bore the crew with my problems. Too much work to do.

Part of the problem I was wrestling with was Kate's safety. I'd told her the flat-out truth that day in Lincoln when I said that the town was a powder keg ready to explode, and she knew it as well as I did. Hell, everybody in Lincoln County knew it! Most of them were just too damn scared to talk much more than they had to about it. Other than those two editors who were still threatening to kill one another and the main participants in the whole affair, of course. But as long as it was only words they were throwing back and forth everything was all right. It's just that someday those words were going to turn into bullets and there wouldn't be any room left for talking of any kind, and I didn't want Kate caught in the cross fire.

Then there was that other thing, the fact that I'd told her I loved her. That was a part of the problem too. As the days went by I began to wonder if I hadn't told her that just to get her to move out here to the Chisum spread. Did I really love her? Did I have any right to love her? I even asked myself if she had any idea of what kind of life she'd be getting into if she hitched up with me, but I already knew the answer to that, and so did she. We'd both been around too long to not know how this land was and what it took to survive in it. Maybe, if you were lucky, you could live a little after you'd survived, but mostly it was a struggle.

I'd seen her, of course, whenever I'd gone into town for supplies, and she'd waited until the store was clear of customers and then flirted some with me, if you can call rushing into my arms flirting, and I'd start asking myself all of those questions again and put them out of my mind quick because . . . well, being with Kate was living, not surviving, and being with her made all of the difference in the world. It was past the middle of July when I saw her and she started acting almost giddy about being with me, nearly reaching over to kiss me when one of the local town gossips was in the store. It gave me the damnedest feeling, being around her that day.

A few days later everything started happening at once.

About noon one day Sonny pulled up in front of the cookshack. It was strange seeing him without Billy the Kid standing there next to him. The two had become constant companions and friends, of that I was sure.

"Where's the Kid?"

"He said he had something to take care of," was his only reply as he dismounted. Then, in a manner that reminded me much of the shy boy who had arrived here over four months ago, he added, "You said to come tell her myself." He shrugged. "I reckon it's about time."

"I'll say." He followed me inside. "Missy, give the man a cup of coffee." She looked up, saw the tall young man behind me who'd done some more filling out, looked surprised as all get out and started running straight at me. Except it wasn't me she was running to. I stepped aside and Sonny took her right into his arms and kissed her. "Well, now, that's one way of saying hello," I said, stepping between them. And from the scowls I got from both of them when I did, why, you'd have thought I should've been refereeing a fight instead of what I did.

"Do you mind if I talk to her *alone*, Dallas?"

"Course not." I looked at her with a devilish eye, then back at Sonny. "You know, she's just as bad as you was. Now I gotta chop all that wood she said she'd have done and don't." I reckon we all knew it was an excuse to let them be alone. "You remember now, missy," I added, walking away, "you got you a pie and a stew that's needing looking after."

"I won't forget, Dallas," she smiled over her shoulder.

I made it to the doorway, then stopped again.

"And children."

"What now, Dallas?" Sonny asked, a bit impatient.

"I don't mind family reunions, but let's don't make this too awful long."

"Family reunions?" both said at almost the same time.

I pushed my hat back, grinned, knowing I'd have to make a quick exit. "Why, sure! I figure if this reunion lasts any too long . . . why, there's sure 'nough gonna be a family comes of it."

Margaret turned pure red in the face and Sonny's John B. went sailing past my head as I stepped out the side entrance. I had a pretty good idea of what they'd be talking about, so I didn't make any effort to stay close to the door. Besides, there was always wood that needed chopping.

I wasn't out there but ten minutes when I heard a rider coming. From a distance I thought I recognized Tom Lang's mount, but the man riding it was too short to have been Lang. Must've loaned out his horse to send Shorty back to the ranch, I thought, remembering that Lang's was one of those mustangs that never failed to win a horse race when they were run. But as the horse and rider neared I saw that it was Tom Lang. He hadn't looked as tall in the saddle as he usually did because he was slumped over in it. And as bloody as he was, he looked like he'd fought a grizzly bear and come out on the short end of it.

I grabbed the reins of the horse as it entered the yard, ready to help the man off, but Lang simply dropped the reins and, using both hands, pushed himself upright in the saddle. His face had been drained of blood, he was that pale, but no wonder for it was all over the front of him!

"What happened, son? Who done it?" were the first words out of my mouth. Out of the corner of my eye I saw Sonny and Margaret coming into the yard, heard the girl gasp at the sight of Tom Lang and knew without having to look that he had tried to shield her from the terrifying sight in the saddle.

"Back shooter . . . that Turk is," he said in a voice that was weak at first. He was a dying man and he knew it and I reckon it was that knowledge that made him put everything he had into those last words. "Them sonsabitches with him are deader'n me though. *Sonny,"* he said, emphasizing the boy's name, "you take care of her . . . do you fine." Then pausing for a moment, his gaze turned back to me and that devil-may-care smile came to his face as the voice weakened again. "Told you, Dallas, 'ride like a Comanch', shoot like a Tenn—' " But he never finished it, falling slowly off his horse. I caught him, helped the man's body to the ground. Why is it people have to die just when you think you're taking a liking to them?

"What did he mean about the ones with Turk Calder?" Sonny asked, still holding Margaret, who had buried her face in his chest and was now crying.

Having blood on me was nothing new, so there was no hesitation when I reached down and pulled out Tom Lang's pistol. I opened the loading gate and slowly ejected three spent cartridges from the chamber of it, held them in my open hand for the boy to see.

"Remember them three who was 'bout to do us in afore you fought Calder a couple of months back? The ones Tom shot the guns outta their hands?" He nodded, remembering as vividly as I did. "My guess is them's the sonsabitches he was talking 'bout." I said it just like he had, not even caring that there was a woman present.

The pie burned. So did the stew. But I didn't really give a damn because I had something more important to take care of.

They say you can measure a man's success in life by the hole that he leaves, so I reckon it doesn't matter where it was that I buried Tom Lang. He had no family that anyone knew of, so I took it upon myself to dig his grave, but it wasn't long before those who actually were loafing around the bunkhouse found me and lent a hand. Margaret did what she could to salvage supper, although I didn't hear anyone complain too loudly to her, and Sonny . . . well, he just disappeared from sight.

I never was much with a Bible and all of those fancy quotes they speak of, but I figure that what I said was as good as any sky pilot could have. It was sunset by then and most of the crew was back, Charlie taking over as the new top screw. Tom Lang had been a hard man but a fair one and you couldn't ask for more than that out in this land. Some of the men had liked him because of that and some hadn't, but it wasn't until I put up the wooden cross that would be his calling card to those who passed by the grave that I found out how private a man Tom Lang had really been. In many ways you can't blame a man for being close-mouthed in this land. Hell, none of us are perfect and a good share of us even less than that, I reckon. So the way it turned out, the only time Tom Lang had done any bragging was that day he'd laid it all out for John Chisum and me, and even that wasn't brag. Not one bit.

"I didn't know that," a lot of the boys said when they glanced at the marker I'd made for the man. Made me wonder why it was that you had to wait for a man to die to show respect that was likely due him when he was alive and more worthy of it.

The marker wasn't much, just some wood nailed together with Tom Lang's name on it and the date 18 July, 1878, as his date of death. I figured the epitaph fit the man: HE RODE WITH BEN MCCULLOCH was burned into the wood and it was this that the crew hadn't known about. Me, I figured it was time they knew.

Yes, Tom Lang had left a big hole to be filled, a mighty big one. And someone, Turk Calder in particular, was going to pay for it. You could bank on it!

CHAPTER EIGHTEEN

The next morning she wasn't at the cookshack when I arrived. Usually, she got there before me and had the fire going good and hot, but this morning my Ben Franklin was colder than Mother Nature in the dead of winter. Probably had a bad night sleeping, I reasoned to myself, for I knew mine had been the same way. I'd let her sleep in this one time.

You get a certain frame of mind when you're a cook. No matter how bad things seem you always have to have food for the men. That is your prime consideration for wherever you're working. Fact is, you'll find a lot of us old biscuit shooters who'll tell you that it was beans more than bullets that kept a man going in this land rather than that fictional pap they fed you in those penny-dreadfuls. Hell, the only thing dreadful about them was the penny you got suckered into spending on them! So I went about my usual chores of preparing the morning meal, but it was the death of Tom Lang that was heavy on my mind as I did it. It must've been the same with the crew because they were eating in relative silence compared to the usual chatter I heard.

It was after they'd gone that I took some coffee over to the main house, figuring I'd wake up Margaret so we could get back to the work at hand. I didn't know where Sonny had taken off to, but it kept crossing my mind that if he brought the Kid in with him next time, why, I'd hire the boy myself just to get Turk Calder hunted down.

"Oh, she's not here," Sallie said calmly, sort of like she knew everything that was going on. "She told me to give

you this." I set the pot of coffee down and grabbed the
paper out of her hands. It had been neatly folded into
quarters. "She said you'd understand."

I opened it up, fumbling nervously with it, knowing it
would come of no good but that I couldn't help it. It was
Margaret's handwriting all right, I'd have recognized it
anywhere.

Dearest Dallas,

Call it woman's intuition if you like, but I fear Sonny
has gone after Turk Calder. I love him, Dallas, the
same way that you love Kate, so please understand that
I must go to him. I believe it's what you call being "one
to ride the river with." If I don't go now, I'll never be
any good for him.

It had that pretty little scrawl underneath that could only
belong to Margaret Dawson.

"GODDAMNIT!" I yelled, throwing the letter on the
table.

"Dallas!" Sallie said, shocked. "How dare—"

"How dare! I'll give you how dare!" I said in not quite so
loud a voice. "She goes after that Dennison boy and Turk
Calder's gonna kill *her* just like he will the boy! Who the
hell do you think it was I buried last night!" Furious didn't
come anywhere close to describing how I felt then, for
truth be known, I'd taken a liking to Margaret Dawson, I
really had. I took that bent up old beaver hat of mine off
and slammed it on the table as Sallie read the letter, her
eyes growing bigger as she did.

"You mean—"

"Can't anyone do nothing right around here?" I asked of
no one in particular, sloshing my hat on and storming out
the door as furious as young Margaret Dawson had once
been.

"Dallas, be careful," I heard Sallie say from the veranda,
but I was halfway across the yard and didn't bother to look

back. Not out of any disrespect or peevishness or anything, you understand. It's just that I had other things on my mind.

I picked the best horse of the lot, the one Jim Chisum had been riding since he'd arrived, and was mounted, my Greener in one hand, shot pouch draped over my shoulder and that old Colt Sonny had taken once, when Jim Chisum came across the yard.

"And just what the hell do you think you're doing?" he asked with the kind of authority that only Uncle John knew how to throw around. Trouble was, I wasn't in the mood for authority, no matter whose it was.

"What's it look like," I said as ornery as I felt, "I'm stealing your horse. You want him back get you a posse up. You'll likely find him someplace in Lincoln."

Then I put my heels to that mount and was gone.

It wasn't so much Sonny I was concerned over as it was the two women. The boy had chosen to ride with Billy the Kid and seemed to have come a long way from that day he'd escorted Margaret Dawson onto the Chisum spread, no more a tall, gangly youngster looking for a way of life. He'd have to fight his own fights now, for once you start packing iron on this side of the Mississippi and calling yourself a man . . . well, you've got to live up to it. And that ain't easy. As far as I knew, the only thing Sonny had going for him was hearing Tom Lang tell how Turk Calder was a back shooter, so if he'd picked up some horse sense along with that gun he was wearing he might watch his back trail.

All of it led to Kate, which is the only reason I rode off that fast in the first place. Those three pilgrims hadn't taken Tom Lang's advice to leave the country and he wound up killing them before he had died as well. And because of that I had a gut feeling that Rope Burn, the man who'd scared the bejesus out of Kate, hadn't taken my advice either. This Seven Rivers Gang was a pretty tough outfit, having had the run of the town of Lincoln since they'd arrived, all at the insistence of the sheriff of Lincoln County, who was a Dolan man anyway. I knew as well as Sonny that Lincoln had become a headquarters for this faction and that it was there he'd find Turk Calder without much looking. I also knew that if Turk Calder was there in Lincoln, so was Rope Burn, and that meant that Kate was in danger. Hell, that was likely the first place Margaret would look, figuring Kate would know where to find Sonny and the Kid!

Me, ride like hell? Not hardly! I rode like there was no tomorrow, and for all I knew it might just be that way.

Later, after it was all over, some said that the sound approaching town was like a buffalo herd. The Regulators, Alexander McSween and Billy the Kid among them, rode in to Lincoln, forty strong. The sheriff and what remained of the Dolan faction came riding in from the other side of town with the same amount of men. All but twelve of the families that lived in Lincoln had been evacuated, knowing that, just like I'd predicted, a powder keg was about to go off. The whole fight had come to a head and would take place in Lincoln.

Long before I could hear the gunfire I could see the smoke, and that only made me urge my mount the more. What if that smoke was coming from the Montano store? What if she'd been hurt? What if . . . I put it all aside, knowing that this was a time for doing, not thinking, and the devil take the hindmost.

When I rode in I felt a sigh of relief when I saw the Montano store still standing. Most of the gunfire was on the far side of town, although a bullet careened off the front of the store as I pulled up before it, jumped from the saddle and gave my horse a whack on the butt. The door was immediately opened for me and I made my way in, Kate and Margaret Dawson the only occupants of the store.

"Are you all right, Dallas?" Kate asked, concerned.

"That was a damn fool thing to do," I said, ignoring her, focusing my ire on Margaret.

"But didn't you get my—"

"Yes, and it was a damn fool thing to do!" I growled. Turning to Kate, I said, "Comes in here looking for Sonny 'cause she can't live without him. Dumb girl get herself killed!"

"No, I won't," she answered defiantly, pulling out a Colt from underneath the buckskin jacket she wore.

"Now, where did you get that?" I took the gun from her, gave it a once-over and knew it was Tom Lang's by the blood still in the grooves of the handle if nothing else. I spun the cylinder, checking to see if it was loaded. There were six beans in the wheel. "Least you loaded it." I handed it back to her. "Now what the hell's going on? Ain't that McSween's place I seen afire when I come in?"

"That's it," Kate said, all business. Romancing was going to have to wait today for the situation was looking serious.

"Well, where's the Kid? Where's Sonny?"

"Probably in that building with McSween and whatever other of his men aren't shooting it out with Dolan's men in this town." From the look on Margaret's face—one of pure shock and horror—I had the feeling this was the first time Kate had mentioned that possibility to the younger girl.

"Oh no!" Margaret said, doom on her face. "They haven't got a chance! They'll be—"

"Killed or burned to death," Kate said, but by then the girl was in my arms, crying. "It must be hell on earth in there now," Kate added. "All Dolan's men have to do is wait for them to try to escape one by one and kill them like so many flies." I had a notion I knew what she was getting at, what this was all leading to.

"Calder or his men been around?"

"No," she replied. "In fact, I'm amazed that no one has tried to enter this place yet."

"Ammunition? Guns?"

"There's ammunition in the back, but the guns are all gone, except for the one Margaret brought in." There was a pause for a moment when I don't think either of us knew what to say.

"I know how to use this, Dallas," Margaret finally said, pulling out Lang's pistol again.

"Decided all of a sudden you want to see ary you'll due to ride the river with, eh?"

"You forget, Dallas," Kate said, "I've been in a shoot-out or two myself." A confused look came to Margaret's face but Kate and I knew what she was talking about. She hadn't lied when she said she knew what that burning McSween building must be like either, of that I was sure. "Do it for me, Dallas. I don't care about the rest. But if you could help Sonny get out . . ." Her voice trailed off and I knew she'd get her way, like all women do with their men.

"Aw, hell!" I said, unbuckling my holster and shell belt and handing them to Kate. "Here, now you got one too. Just make sure you put 'em to good use ary trouble comes afore I get back."

"Of course." Kate kissed me and somehow it made me feel I'd be all right, that I'd survive to see her again.

I worked my way across the street to the back of the Baca Corral and past the Tunstall store, where three of McSween's sharpshooters were stationed. They were about the only ones who hadn't pot-shotted me, the only reason I'd made it that far being that not too many people care for that loud boom a ten-gauge Greener makes when it goes off. The sound is enough to scare the hell out of you, and if you know that double ought buckshot is likely coming at you along with it, well, friend, it has a real telling effect on just how brave you are at the moment.

The building was in flames all right! I don't think I've ever seen such a huge fire in my life. The windows were all shot out or busted out and how the structure was still standing was a miracle to me, for its entirety seemed engulfed in flames. The only thing that could've been alive in there was the devil himself and he was likely stoking the fire. But even as I thought it I was proved wrong again.

The Kid came rushing out the back door to the kitchen, standing there for one instant, trying to get his bearings, I reckon. I've been out in the desert a time or two and I know what heat can do to you. Bake you on the outside and fry your innards while it's at it, it will.

I was way the hell out of range, but I saw one of Dolan's men take a stance on that back wall before the Kid saw him, and let go with one barrel of my Greener. That got his attention and he pot-shotted me while the Kid shot him. Then that sawed-off runt of a gunman was running toward me like it was the foot race of his life and I let go of that second barrel before another sharpshooter could target him. By the time he got to me I was reloading my shotgun and the three sharpshooters of McSween's were covering us as Billy did the same.

"Where's Sonny? You seen him around?"

Before I could answer I saw a tall figure fly through one of the window frames head first, do a somersault, come to his feet and make tracks for the two of us.

"I do believe that's him," the Kid smiled while all of this took place. Both were hatless, their clothes singed in various places. Sonny looked serious as could be, but the Kid still had a sense of humor, although I was beginning to wonder if it wasn't just a mite perverted after what he'd been through. I couldn't see how anyone could enjoy that kind of torture.

"Kate's needing help," I said.

"Not a chance," was the Kid's immediate reply. "I'm killing off as many of this Dolan and Seven Rivers Gang as I can." He gave me a brief smile. "Ain't that often you get 'em all in one place for a turkey shoot," he added, by way of explanation, I reckon, then he was gone.

"I'm going with him," Sonny said before I could explain

that his girl was in the Montano store with Kate, then he was gone as well.

That meant fighting my own way back to Kate without any of the help I'd figured I'd be able to get, and that wasn't all that healthful because one of those coyotes gave me a flesh wound in the arm.

There was so much shooting and black powder filling the air that I wasn't sure I saw some movement across the street before I ran to Kate's store, or whether I was imagining I'd seen it. I was halfway across the street when I heard another shot from inside Kate's store. The door was open and I ran to it, my shotgun at the ready. Two dead men were to the side of the entrance, but what distressed me most was the sight of Kate, laying there face down on the floor, a bullet hole in her back. I leaned the Greener up against the counter, slowly turning her over. She still had some life in her, but a pool of blood was quickly forming underneath her.

"It would've been a boy," she said, trying to smile through all the pain. I gave a quick glance at her midsection, noticed ever so slight a bulge below her waistline, knew at once why she had been so giddy that last time. She was with child and it was mine. "Looks like Tom was right," she said softly but it was too late. In my arms now was a dead woman, likely the only woman I'd ever really loved in my life.

I wasn't conscious of the rest of the world then, concerned only about my own world which had just fallen to pieces. A couple of tears rolled down my cheeks as I looked at her in my arms, wondering how I'd ever live again, or if I'd even care. Then the killing mad in me reached a boiling point and her last words ran through my mind—"Looks like Tom was right"—and in an instant I knew what she'd meant. No one needed to tell me that Turk Calder had back shot her just as he had Tom Lang. And I knew I wouldn't have to hunt him down, for when I looked up there he was. Rope Burn was with him and four new cronies he'd picked up, likely from the Seven Rivers Gang. But it was Calder who stood out among them all, one of his big arms wrapped around Margaret Dawson who he held in front of him as a shield, his pistol pointed at the side of her head.

"I've about had enough of you Seven Rivers sonsabitches," I said, mean and hard, setting Kate's body down slowly and grasping my Greener as I stood up. They could have done me in, as deliberate as my moves were, but they didn't, for their attention had focused now on the two men who'd stepped into the store and taken up places, one on each side of me. Billy the Kid on the left and Sonny on the right. And I don't mind telling you I was relieved and surprised at the same time.

"Now that you mention it, I have too," the Kid said, the playfulness gone from his voice. "Ain't none of these Seven Rivers scum I ever met who knew who his daddy was." You couldn't find much more eloquent a way to call a man a bastard.

Out of the corner of my eye I noticed that Sonny had immediately drawn his pistol when he saw Margaret standing there, horrified as could be, and had it pointed at arm's length with Turk Calder in his sights.

"Let her go, Turk, or I'll kill you where you stand." No fooling around, no bluffing, just plain old blunt talk. By God, the boy might make it out here yet. If we got out of this scrape, that is.

"Thought you went hunting Seven Rivers men," I said, cocking both barrels of my shotgun, not sure what was about to happen. I was already responsible for Kate's death, so you can be sure I wasn't about to be held responsible for Margaret Dawson's killing too! I was madder than hell, but we were in a tight spot that just wouldn't work loose.

"I was," the Kid replied. "Then I remember telling Kate

that I owed her one, so me and Sonny come a-running. Always pay my debts, cookie."

"Got here a mite too late, son. Mebbe ary you'd come along afore it moughta helped, but not now." Saying it just got me all the madder and I had an intense urge to open the ball and end the whole damn thing. But there was Calder holding a gun to Margaret's head.

"You're the ones that better be dropping the guns," Turk said with what I thought was a tad of nervous in the tone of his voice. "I got nothing to lose." He pressed the gun harder against her skull.

"Dallas, please," she pleaded.

"Hell," I said in disgust, "I thought you was one to ride the river with! Just a spoiled goddamn Easterner after all." That brought the fire to her eyes and she got that defiant look again.

"The Kid teach you how to use that thing, Sonny?" It was all total silence now, none of us sure who was going to do what or to whom.

"Just the basics, Dallas," he said, his gun still trained on Turk. "Never carry a gun less'n you aim to use it; never pull it out less'n you aim to shoot, and don't shoot less'n it's to kill."

Rope Burn couldn't cut much more of this and showed it.

"You can go to hell," he said, and that tore it!

"I already been there, you dirty sonofabitch, and I'm making it your next stop."

That was the last of the talking that was done. I leveled the Greener at Rope Burn and pulled one trigger, the charge sending him flying back into a gun rack as his chest poured blood and vitals onto the floor. My second blast got the man next to him in the same place, but not before he'd put a slug in my shoulder.

Margaret brought her foot down on Turk's and he let out a scream, pulling his gun away from her head long enough for Sonny to place a head shot that guaranteed he was dead before he hit the floor.

I'd have swore I only heard one shot, but those three hombres on my left facing the Kid were dead when I looked. Once again, Billy the Kid had come through the scrape without a cut. That boy had the damnedest luck.

"Sonny!" I yelled, hearing more of them coming in through the back entrance even before I saw them. I had no pistol and my shotgun was now useless, its loads spent.

Three of them rushed through the doorway, spraying lead every which way. The same three died there, gunned down by what remained of the three each shells that Billy and Sonny used up on them. Then it got silent as the echo of the gunfire died down, both inside and out, and the smoke cleared the air.

Margaret rushed into Sonny's arms, holding to him for dear life.

"Sure took you long enough," I growled.

"Huh?" The boy looked at me, puzzled.

"Hell, boy, you finally did something right! Now someone find me a doctor afore I bleed to death."

"And some tequila," the Kid added.

CHAPTER NINETEEN

"Will I ever see you again?" It was a week later. Kate had been given a proper funeral, Lincoln had settled down and tried to go back to its normal way of life and most of the outlaw element had left the town—if not the territory—for good. I had my arm in a sling and could talk of nothing but moving on, and Margaret kept telling me that I belonged on the Chisum spread. Maybe so, may not. All I knew was that what they were calling the Lincoln County War was far from over and whether I belonged with Uncle John or not I didn't consider it my war. I'd gotten too close to a woman, had grown to love her, only to be the cause of her death. That didn't set right with me so I figured it was time to move on.

"Don't know, darlin'," I said. "Mountains was always a cure-all for anything ailed me. You and Sonny get up there, mebbe you can look me up."

They were ready to mount up, a pack mule holding all they must've needed or figured to. When I left I wouldn't even need that, as little as I had. But they were going and it was together so at least things had worked out for them.

"It wasn't your fault, you know," she said.

"I know that, darlin', but it's like I told you oncet. Them hearts got a mind of their own and they take a long time to heal." I gave her a hug, winced when she put too much pressure on the sling my arm was in, then kissed her forehead. "Don't you worry, missy, I'll be all right."

They forked those saddles before Sonny looked down at me.

"What did you mean that day when you said I finally did something right, Dallas?" It wasn't an idle question, rather one that he wanted an honest answer to, so I gave him one.

"Why, you stood up to 'em, son, stood up for *her*, stood up like a man should." I paused, smiled. "Mebbe I shouldn't be calling you Sonny no more."

"Oh, I don't know," he replied, "I sort of like it."

"Where you headed?"

"I'm not sure," he shrugged. "I'm not cut out for cooking, and I sure ain't a farmer or a cattleman. I never did tell you, Dallas, but I did some reading in those law books before I came out here. Who knows, maybe some sheriff or marshal needs a deputy out here. There sure does seem like enough lawlessness in the territory."

"Mought be, son, you mought just have the makings." I meant that and they both knew it. "Whatever it is, you take care of her," I added, nodding toward Margaret, "or I'll come and show you how the Crow lift a topknot."

"You bet, Dallas," he smiled. "You know, for being a crusty old codger, I could take a liking to you."

They were walking their mounts halfway across the yard when I called out "Sonny!"

"Yeah, Dallas."

"Get to a town that's got a sky pilot so's you can marry that girl afore you get her in trouble!"

"Dallas," Margaret said, turning in the saddle and blushing, "where do you think I'm taking him?"

Just like a woman. One way or another they'll get you.

ABOUT THE AUTHOR

Jim Miller began his writing career at age ten when his uncle presented him with his first Zane Grey novel. A direct descendant of Leif Erickson and Eric the Red, and a thirteen-year Army veteran, Mr. Miller boasts that stories of adventure flow naturally in his blood. When not writing, Mr. Miller spends his time ensconced in his 2,000-volume library filled mostly with history and research texts on the Old West. The author lives in Aurora, Colorado, with his wife and their two children.